# Totally
# Toasted

To Marnie Dickson and the Mongrel Mob ...
Don't be buggin' me at this address. And no calls.

PANTS ON FIRE PRESENTS ...

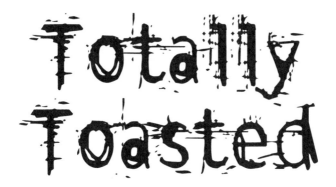

# Totally Toasted

Paul Stafford

A special thank you to Amanda Woodbine,
who gave me the title for this book

 **Pants on Fire**

An imprint of
Crawford House Publishing Pty Ltd
PO Box 1484
Bathurst NSW 2795, Australia

First published by Crawford House Publishing, 1999

Illustrations and cover painting by Shane Summerton
Back cover photograph by David H. Barrett

National Library of Australia Cataloguing-in-Publication entry
    Stafford, Paul, 1966- .
        Totally toasted.

        ISBN 1 86333 177 8.

        I. Title.  II. Title: Pants on fire presents – Totally toasted.

    A823.3

Printed in Australia

10   9   8   7   6   5   4   3   2   1
08   07   06   05   04   03   02   01   00   99

# Contents

# Special Thanks

To Stick Barrett, editor, neighbour and horse whisperer, for services to Team Pants above and beyond the call of duty. Eternal gratitude to my best mate and mentor, George E. Peterson, an avowed westie, for guidance through the minefield. To Shane Summerton, problem child, Jarrod 'Why'd ya do it?' McCauley, Dave 'Pug-whisky' Currall, and Tony and Jen Crawford, for believing in the project. Also to the Very Reverend Gerry Candlearse for spiritual guidance (which I ignored), and Jim and Judy Rutherford, for renting me a piece of Paradise.

# Anthony Kerr and the Subtracter Factor

Anthony Kerr had ackers like Saturn has sunspots on its ring – masses. He had cheeks like a greasy focaccia, with extra lumps of dried tomatoes and diced jalapeño peppers and sour clotted cream. His face was a meal in itself, though not one any sane nutritionalist would recommend.

Anthony had Zits Twelve, even though the measuring equipment only went up to ten. He never went near mirrors because he didn't need reminding that his crater-face look was a spitting double for the man in the moon.

No, Anthony Kerr didn't need any reminders, but he was constantly reminded anyway. People just wouldn't leave him or his ackers alone. Busybodies and nosy neddies were his downfall. They made his life complete hell.

Society was to blame, yet again.

See, nobody else in Anthony's hometown of Stapleton had ackers. They sorta missed them. That's why they bugged Anthony. Everyone considered those ackers *their* ackers too, and wanted news, news and more news concerning Anthony Kerr's facial status.

Anthony was so over it he was under it, and really starting to despair. Why him? Why should he alone, out of all the residents of Stapleton, suffer the curse of such acutely accelerated ackerfication?

Technically he knew the reason why. A year ago he'd accidentally slipped on an acne curse smeared around a public toilet seat by a wayward warlock. The misanthropic magician reckoned it'd be a real funny joke for one boy in a town of a thousand greasy teenagers to inherit the burden of all their acne, plus his own.

Ask Anthony about it. Some joke. Real funny.

So now, after wearing the weight of Stapleton's festering face-fungus for a full foul year, the 'funny' joke was wearing very freakin' thin. It was sending Anthony broke, for one thing. He'd done every scrub, rub, and drug known to science, with no discernible physical effect except a dramatic loss of weight around his wallet area.

He'd tried meditation, mediation, reconciliation, and spiflication, but none of those expensive processes was worth a pinch of pus. He'd even resorted to consulting the local voodoo doctor, with thoroughly dubious results.

But nothing worked …

Everyone has problems. Some people have cancer in their toes, and some people have white moth in their cabbages. Everyone has problems. Anthony's problem was parenthood.

Anthony was the single surrogate parent of all the ackers in Stapleton. He didn't have a choice, and all the other greasers who should've been zit-ridden were happy about it. They loved not having to tote, feed and water their own acne, and instead watch Anthony Kerr do it for them. But, outrageously, they still wanted access to 'their children' – they still wanted visiting rights to their old zits. It was like a father who, despite paying no maintenance, still demanded his kids on weekends.

Everyone in Stapleton took an enthusiastic interest in the lurid, constantly evolving canvas of Anthony Kerr's face. Everyone wanted constant updates on Anthony's ackers, a blow-by-blow account of each and every birth.

Just brewing a blind lumper with no puseous head to speak of caused riotous outbreaks of celebrations and merriment in the ranks of Stapleton citizens, so you can appreciate how a handsome-headed zit was an absolute hit, and a Siamese twin put them in a spin.

A Siamese twin (as it's tagged in the trade) occurs when two custardy heads grow out of the same thumper zit. They were a glorious and horrifying sight – rarer than rocking-horse shit – so when Anthony cranked out three of them two weeks in a row, Stapleton went completely berserk.

It upset the poor kid mightily. Wasn't the acker plague bad enough? Couldn't they just leave him alone?

Anthony begged them. All he wanted was a bit of privacy. But no. Not them.

Anthony considered it very bad style for Mike Moron on 'A Current Affray' to splash an 'acne exposé' all over the nation's TV screens prime-time, making out the boy was basically long-haired, shifty and work-shy, then label the special report 'Simple Pimple!'

Anthony thought it wholly unnecessary for the Macquarie Dictionary to define the term 'pimple-faced' with the reference 'see Anthony Kerr'.

And he regarded it majorly out of order when the Australian Acne Club posted his photograph on its web-site with the title '*Lifetime President A. Kerr, F.A.C.E.*'

A. Kerr. Acker. Yes. Very amusing. At least the other forty-five hundred thousand acne-club members thought so when they saw it. They rejoiced in the knowledge that although they had problem skin with ackers, Anthony's problem was *finding* skin between the ackers.

The boy was wall-to-wall pluke, Luke.

If there was one thing in his life Anthony wished he could reverse it was his horrible harvest of ackers. He wished and wished, but wishing did him no good. He'd tried all that trippie-hippie stuff. He'd had a gutful of wishing wells, magic spells, voodoo bells, dud advice from interfering rels, donations to Saint Kells (patron saint of the spotty), and every other variation of chowder-brained superstitious nonsense known to man or braying beast.

Anthony tried them all – every single one – but nothing even bordered on budging the blight of blotches on his bodgie bonce. Not even a sustained Stinger-missile strike could've shifted Anthony Kerr's ackers.

They bit. Ackers, that is. Biting didn't get rid of them

though. Anthony had tried that too. He'd once bound his face with a bandage squirming with biting maggots, to slurp away all the surplus sludge suspended across his vile dial.

The maggot bandages were the latest thing in highbrow medico circles, used by trendy doctors to suck the muck from those oozing, festy tropical ulcers that stubbornly refuse to heal. Those maggoty little suckers worked a charm on tropical ulcers, top of the list of unshiftable maladies. You'd think they'd shift ackers, surely.

But the maggots didn't take to Anthony Kerr's face at all. There was nothing even remotely tropical about that boy's acne, and the maggots couldn't be fooled into action, even after Anthony slapped coconut oil and pinacolada flavoured sunscreen all over the drop zone.

The maggot bandage was a desperate act, but these were desperate times. Anthony had made several serious attempts to suction the sickly slime from his oil-slick face, with suck-all success.

Nothing had worked. There was nothing left to try …

So now you get the general gist. Anthony was ready to give up – half-mad with grief, stricken with despair, paralysed with dread, kibbled with rye, and yet still just stupid enough to try one last, not necessarily safe, completely quack cure.

As he read the dodgy ad in the weekend newspaper, Anthony was thoroughly aware of who was who and what was what – he was looking at his *last* chance, and he knew it. Modern medicine, traditional medicine, herbal medicine and even voodoo medicine had all failed him. So, inevitably, he drifted to quantum mathematics.

Call it crapola, but this bit is true. In one of the dowdier suburbs bordering Stapleton, there resided a mad scientist who dabbled in quantum mathematics. That in itself is news, considering the generally boring species of dude hangin' in the 'burbs. But wait – there's more. The mad scientist's craziness credentials were all in order – prior to branching into mad science he'd gone bust doing a home-delivery pizza run, and you've got to be a state-registered loony to even dip your toe in those greasy, cholesterol-laden waters.

But the mad scientist did.

After a string of rotten experiences in the fast-food industry, dozens of fake orders from bogus addresses, and seven hundred and forty-nine straight nights of pizza for dinner, the mad scientist vowed to return to his lab one more time. He vowed he'd have one last shot at his life-time's failed pet project – the subtracter beam. And he vowed he'd never eat pizza again.

He stuck at it for several months with little or no suc-cess, apart from the not-eating-pizza bit, which he achieved easily, by shifting to a one hundred per cent steak diet. But no matter what the scientist added to the subtracter beam mix, or how he twiddled the adjusters and adjusted the twiddlers on the circuit board, the result was always the same – substantially less than bugger all, measured on standard laboratory equipment.

Finally – bankrupt, dejected, disheartened and solidly constipated by his relentless red-meat diet – the mad scientist broke down. It happened on a really busy high-way, and he cursed and bashed at the wheel as he steered his stricken car onto the side of the road. This was all he needed – car-repair bills.

A beaten up yellow Holden pulled up in front of him. A young woman in greasy overalls slid out, and came towards him smiling. She was a mechanic, on her way to work. She fiddled around for a bit, got the mad scientist's car started, and explained the problem was in the carby, but could easily be repaired.

'It wants to run but it's getting too much fuel. Gotta cut back a bit. Rather than adding more ingredients, it's better to subtract in this kind of equation.'

These words hit the mad scientist like a brick in the brain. Of course! He'd been approaching the subtracter-beam problem from exactly the wrong end – he was trying to fuel his subtracter beam by *adding* things when he should've been *subtracting*, with the obvious disappointing results.

Fool of a man!

The mad scientist raced home, ignoring red lights, stop signs and even zebras crossing – mad scientists see that kind of nonsense all the time, but soon learn to zen it out.

Once in the lab, instead of adding all his parts together and blowing off a bit of stinky steam in the blue tubes, the mad scientist *subtracted* it all. He subtracted three parts pure quantum maths, a jigger-and-a-bit of second-hand high-school physics, discarded a bunch of stuff that had been rattling around his top drawer for years, and very calmly, very quietly, very collectedly, finally cracked that exceedingly mad and retrospectively regrettable invention – the infamous Candlearse Subtracter Beam.

Hosanna!

Now Dr Gerry Candlearse, mad scientist, was barking keen to use his invention. He took out a seven-line ad in the paper, and filled all seven lines with complete, one hundred per cent, certifiable gibberish.

His subtracter beam, Candlearse claimed in the cheapo, grainy newspaper advertisement, actually accessed a perpetual keyhole into the exciting parallel universe that exists and thrives exactly alongside our own tedious one. Applied judiciously, the beam could subtract anything from this universe and shot-put it into the parallel universe, safe and sound, out-of-sight-out-of-mind, gone, vamoose! Pot bellies, unwanted facial hair, excess earage, mothers-in-law – what you don't miss you never regret. So get rid of it! Now! Don't delay! Mention this ad for a five per cent discount!

And so on.

The ad rumbled along with this and other unsubstantiated and generally dangerous claims, and the overwhelmingly high-strung tone of the piece served its purpose perfectly – everyone who read it dismissed it as the crazed work and unstable lunacy of a genuinely mad scientist, to be avoided at all costs.

Everyone except Anthony Kerr, that is.

The list in the advert claiming effectiveness 'in all these areas' included zits.

Enter Anthony.

The mad scientist was beaverishly eager to get Anthony's business – the newspaper ad had eaten the last of his money, and he desperately needed customers. He also knew Anthony's oldies were loaded, so when the boy came mooching around inquiring about some overdue acne subtraction, the mad scientist jumped that on action and no mistake.

The mad scientist conducted Anthony around the lab.

The subtracter beam was set up on a concrete block, channelled through a mirrored lens, down a pipe, through a funnel, and over a mass of mixed-up wires that buzzed and flashed and constantly short-circuited themselves.

Finally the result came out the other side, a pencil-thin shaft of very white light, buzzing and pulsating and humming with pure energy. The beam had been first refracted, then quadruply enacted, so whatever it hit would be instantly subtracted, and banished to the parallel universe.

Or so the mad scientist reckoned.

Anthony scratched his head. If he ever wanted a zit-free head he had no choice. He *had* to try. Nothing ventured, nothing gained. What else could he do? He just had to subtract those ackers …

Scene: the mad scientist's mad-looking lab. Test tubes and Bunsen burners, stacks of journals and open books of incomprehensible figures. The remains of fourteen or twenty half-eaten steak dinners shrivelled on plates in rock-hard pools of dried tomato sauce linger about as stark testimony to stressful work, late nights, and a diet all Hindus are bound to be unhappy about.

Anthony is strapped, upright, pinioned to a steel girder in the centre of the concrete bunker. The subtracter beam is positioned directly in front of him, its long lens aimed at his face. The expression on his minestrone-ish mug is half hope, half horror.

The switch is flicked!

Everything goes black ...

There are a lot of dangerously ignorant people in the world. Many of them hang around in clusters talking educatedly about stuff they know nowt about. One particularly nauseating cluster consists of a bunch of inbred-nutty academic no-hopers who reckon they know every last thing about parallel universes. They reckon they've sussed the whys, wherefores, and weights (in kilos, microns, or even imperial pounds) of the parallel universe, and insist on extolling their wisdom whenever there's a lull in conversation, whether it's on the bus or in the betting shop.

Thing is, they knew nothing. They were wrong.

The parallel universe, as Anthony Kerr soon discovered, was an entirely different kettle of fish to what the so-called experts and eggkopf-meisters figured it to be.

But hang on – we're getting savagely ahead of ourselves here. How in the name of King Solomon's fattest and sweatiest eunuch would Anthony Kerr *himself* know anything about parallel universes? His ackers might – if the subtraction process had worked – but Anthony himself?

Impossible.

When he rang the mad scientist's number and visited the lab, home of the subtracter beam, Anthony Kerr had but one solid purpose in mind – to rid himself of his loathsome ackers. His plan was simple – pay the mad scientist bloke whatever he asked for, just so long as the subtracter beam did what it claimed to do in the advert.

If that beam subtracted Anthony's ackers from his face and shafted them sideways into the parallel universe (to float and congeal and generally slick their way about the place), then Anthony was happy to pay just about any amount, in any acceptable currency, be it Australian dollars, krugerrand, or even South Sea cowries.

That poor desperate boy would've paid *anything*. He would've sold his soul to Satan if necessary to be free of ackers, but this isn't that kind of story, fortunately.

Unfortunately, the subtracter beam missed. That's to say, it didn't exactly hit a bullseye. Which means, in essence, that it hit but it didn't. It missed, but only what it was aiming for. It did the job, but not the right job.

The subtracter beam couldn't be blamed – it did its bit alright. It surged right into Anthony Kerr's face, full steam ahead, obeying the exact instructions its programmer had punched in – remove the scrofulous surface of Anthony Kerr's festering face. Trouble was, the beam wrongly interpreted the face. It should've taken the grots and left the rest.

It took the rest.

The ackers on Anthony Kerr's face had such a torturous grip on their territory that they were able to claim complete ownership, and exert ownership rights. It was like those weird squatting laws in vacant houses – if you hang there long enough, and there's enough of you, and you make a bit of an effort and plant out a window box with geraniums or some such trifle, then the joint's yours.

So it was with Anthony Kerr's ackers. He no longer owned his face. They did. So when the subtracter beam was kicked into action, and forced to make a choice as to which party to remove and subtract, it wasn't the ackers that went. It was Anthony.

Which is how Anthony Kerr came to be the first certified expert on parallel universes. Suddenly he was in one.

So listen up. Here's the dirt on the parallel universe, and don't get yourself in too much of a lather because there's bugger all to it.

Ask Anthony Kerr.

The parallel universe theorists seemed to believe that the parallel universe was occupied by parallel doubles of everything in this universe, only mirror opposites, whatever in blazes that meant. That talk was obviously double-distilled bollocks of the most cheap and pungent variety, and Anthony Kerr would tell you that straight.

He'd been there. He'd seen it.

The parallel universe, as far as Anthony could ascertain, was just a repository for all those vague, nearly-but-not-quite factors in life, things that might have been but weren't, minor details that hadn't come to pass.

Like, for instance, if you *hadn't* binned that bright yellow, short-sleeve 'casual' nerd shirt Aunty Freda gave you at Christmas, and instead wore it every day of your life, and then got beaten up by some gang every day of your life, on account of that yellow shirt.

Because you *did* bin the shirt, chances are your identical double in the parallel universe wore it, and would be generally beaten and bruised, and limping about in a bloodstained yellow nerd-shirt.

And lucky it wasn't you.

Or, as another example, what about that walrus-style moustache you'd always schemed about growing, but hadn't? Chances are your parallel-universe double *did* grow it. And then chances are he got that job as an undercover cop on account of that fine new walrus-style moustache, and subsequently up and got himself shot in a violent stake-out involving Mexican gunrunners and Sudanese whisky merchants.

Then your parallel-universe double would have a fine walrus-style moustache, and a job with a gun and handcuffs. And be dead.

You get the picture.

But let's get back to Stapleton, in the other universe, where things were out of control. The town had gone near crazy with joy. Dr Candlearse, mad scientist, was being feted as a hero and a genius, for the first time in his life. And he liked it.

The town liked it too. They hadn't realised it before, but they'd always been fonder of Anthony Kerr's ackers than of Anthony Kerr himself.

Now Anthony Kerr's ackers were orphaned. Their only parent had vanished. They were destitute. The people of

Stapleton had to do something. Stapleton would have to adopt Anthony Kerr's ackers. They would become wards of the state.

That suited everyone just fine. Now, with Anthony Kerr out of the way, the good citizens could get all the access they wanted to those ackers, to love and covet and worship them in their own sweet time. The town dug it. There was no Anthony Kerr to slam the door in their faces, or make rude finger signals in a vain effort to drive them away and stop them invading his privacy.

No more of that – no sir! Any good citizen could see those ackers any time, day or night, and for no charge either. They were in heaven.


When the mad scientist's experimental subtracter beam had inadvertently subtracted Anthony instead of his ackers, Dr Candlearse found himself in a tricky situation. Beyond tricky, even. Nasty.

Anthony was gone. Only his shoes remained, and they badly needed cleaning, overflowing as they were with all the loose juice from Anthony's face. The only thing that had lived through the fatal experiment was Anthony Kerr's ackers.

Even the scientist – mad as a bush ant as he was – realised that things had become suddenly very serious. Due to his failed experiment, Anthony was missing, presumed extinct. The boy had parents who probably loved him and would miss him, despite his acne. They would complain, and kick up a stink, sure as. Then things would get legal.

Candlearse was right. Things did get legal. Stapleton Council passed a law declaring a holiday, another law paying the Kerr parents a whack of taxpayers' money in compensation for their ex-son, and then enacted an obscure by-law to immediately build a lush pad in which to house the late Anthony Kerr's ackers, accessible to the public twentyfour seven, for as long as the grasses grow and rivers flow.

The council proclaimed it a red-letter day, and prophesied that Anthony Kerr's ackers would prove to be Stapleton's biggest tourist attraction ever!

Meanwhile, back in the parallel universe, Anthony Kerr was meeting his parallel double. It was a weird moment in science. Here, before his very eyes, was Anthony's what-might-have-been parallel double. And he didn't have an acker on his face. Not one. The boy, Anthony Kerr Two, was as free of zits as a professionally toilet-trained house ferret. Not a pimple anywhere.

There wasn't room, not a single square millimetre spare. Not between all those warts. Could any person alive grow more warts on their head than this bloke? Unlikely.

For one thing, the whole experience made Anthony grateful for *his* situation. Ackers were bad, but at least he'd grow out of them, when his hormones kicked in proper and the bumfluff sprouted meekly from his chin.

But you don't get rid of warts so easy. You don't outgrow warts. Those mongrels hang with you through good times and bad, for richer or poorer, through thick and thin. When it comes to long term commitment, nothing compares to a wart for loyalty.

Anthony Kerr was glad all over that he wasn't the one in the parallel universe, and said as much. Then he and Anthony Kerr Two got in a fight when Two said that Anthony's was the parallel universe and *his* was the real and original one. The whole altercation flared up quickly then, since they were equally matched in wits and strength, and it probably would've ended in a savage bout of fisti-cuffs if the cat hadn't intervened.

The cat was a tabby mongrel pet of the mad scientist. It was old and cranky and losing its marbles. It daydreamed it was in a public cat-toilet when it was perched on the subtracter beam. It pissed all over the dodgy wiring.

There was a great blue flash! *Crack*! The cat was illumi-nated X-ray style for two or three seconds. Two or three million volts (and a not inconsiderable level of amps) surged through it, charging it up like a small sun. Tendrils of white lightning-fire shot from its claws, and its eye-balls spun like an unlucky poker machine.

The cat had made a foolish and ill-conceived choice of place to take a slash. Its parallel-universe double would probably never have to make that choice at all, maybe living somewhere among desert dunes, in a giant sandbox.

That seemed to be the way things worked with the parallel universe, but hey, I'm no expert.

Ask Anthony Kerr, the true expert. Ask him and he'd answer you, because he was back!

The cat's accident had short-circuited the subtracter beam and sent it into rapid reverse. As a result Anthony

Kerr was back, one hundred per cent back in this universe, safe and sound.

The cat was cactus.

But who cares about some lavatorially-challenged cat? Anthony Kerr was back, and back *sans* ackers. *Sans* means 'without', and without them he was, since how could they be on his face when they were now housed in a hyperluxurious, hygienically sealed, public place of worship? Those ackers couldn't be two places at once, could they?

No way. The spell that bound them commanded them to adhere to the victim's face, in this case Anthony's. Now that he was back in the universe the ackers began to experience an excruciating magnetic pull. Their spell bound them to obey the call of Anthony's cleanskin face, but they were imprisoned, trapped, securely lodged behind triple-thickness, tinted, bulletproof glass, with every luxury laid on. It was mega comfortable by any pimple's standards, but the ackers couldn't have left if they'd wanted to.

The magnetic pull became stronger when Anthony was near. And he made sure he was when the first bus-load of loud nosy tourists came through to visit the acker attraction and laugh their heads off at his previous misfortune.

The tourists had eaten heaps of junk food and been jiggled across bad roads in a rattletrap bus called a luxury tourist coach before being dumped in front of the acne enclosure.

Then, right on cue, Anthony appeared.

The ackers felt his presence as if by bat radar. Tendrils of scout ackers slimed up the glass prison walls like a mucus octopus. Anthony stepped closer. Yes! the scouts reported back. Yes! Our long-lost master! Here at last, to claim us back!

The mass of ackers slooped forward as one foul entity, an immense yellowish-greenish jellyfish of microbial wrongness. Slowly, disgustingly, it oozed its way up the glass like a huge poisonous slug. Its toxic, grey-flecked gelatinous mass pulsed with excitement, and if it'd had a tail it would've wagged it and drooled like the happiest hound in the town.

Of course, by now the tourists were ralphing up big-style, yakking in bins and gardens and handbags and on hubbies. The smell of plastic hamburger bile filled the air, and the unhappy tourists filed back onto the bus, leaving a lot lighter than when they arrived.

Which meant they missed the last bit of the performance – Anthony Kerr dancing around in front of his former ackers, prancing delightedly like a loon in June, and not giving a dressmaker's toss who saw him.

The acker bulk jiggled like a giant jelly, keeping time with Anthony's dancing. It was a truly grand finale, a real *coup de grâce*, but few observers – apart from aficionados – would have been able to stomach it to the very end.

And why shouldn't Anthony Kerr celebrate? Finally he had shaken his accursed ackers. Nobody would begrudge him that pleasure, after all he'd been through ...

It wasn't a completely happy ending, though. When the acker subtraction process worked out all OK in the end, a hundred per cent success, the mad scientist suddenly wanted three million dollars payment from Anthony.

Three million bucks! Anthony couldn't pay him. His oldies wouldn't cough up that much either, no way, no how, not for no zits. They laughed out loud at the suggestion. They'd love their son with or without grots. And they'd love that three million bucks just as much, and maybe more, and no way was no mad scientist getting it.

So the mad scientist got even madder, gave Anthony two black eyes and a big fat lip, and sloped off with the boy's brand-new mountain bike and his basketball shoes.

But you get that …

# Pissed Off!

Of course I can't remember the first time I wet the bed. What sort of question is that? Everybody starts life wetting the bed – the *only* thing babies do is swill it in one end and squirt it out the other, yet people fawn and coo and go on with goo-goo noises as if the rug rat overflowing onto their lap is pulling off some noble and highly original act.

So, let's be agreed on that point – *everyone* pisses the bed, some time. Toddlers get a taste for it in nappies, rock on through the pilchers stage, filling their plastic thunderbags like water balloons, then occasionally hang a wetty through their PJs. And then they get bladder control, and the bed-wetting stops.

Only mine never stopped.

Let's get one thing straight from the start – there's nothing *funny* about pissing the bed. Apart from the obvious aspects of grossness and major embarrassment, there's the lesser-known conditions suffered by chronic bed-wetters – urine burn, which is far more painful than sunburn, and insomnia, which is guaranteed.

Insomnia is sleep deprivation, and that's what happens when you try to rack up the zeds in a pool of whizz. It's like falling asleep in the bath – easy when the bath is fresh and warm, but when the contents turn arctic you're sure to wake up in a state of shock.

Then there's the ever-present aroma of *eau de toilet*, French for toilet water, which I'm informed by reliable sources is sold for huge prices in posh dress shops. I mean, how dumb are those purchasers? Does it not say, clearly on the label, 'Toilet Water'? It does. It says it, clear as day, yet those desert-headed dames delicately sprinkle toilet tinkle all over themselves, and pay lots of lolly for the pleasure.

So what's the big deal then? What I do is worth money – big money.

You can call me Miss Piss if you want (which is what my older brother calls me whenever we're out of ear-shot of the oldies), but if you do I'll shuttle you straight into the same category as him – complete bastard.

My real name is Rachael, and I have to say I prefer it. My bro thinks his nickname for me is in some way clever, and that's he's an intellectual giant, but he's wrong – he is merely a giant pain in the gluteus maximus. He really thinks he's some kind of hero, because he's a yuppie who earns a million bucks a year.

He's so on himself that he can't see how pathetic he looks hassling a thirteen-year-old girl. He seems to think making me look small will bolster his image as a big man.

His name is Robert, or Rob the knob. He's fifteen

years older than me, which, as I understand these things to work, means my oldies were on the job even in their wrinkly forties. That's a concept I don't even want to consider, so let's not go there at all.

Anyway, I've got somewhere heaps better to take you – a little jaunt through some lush country known as Revenge Land, where older brothers are fooled up prime-time, and youngest sisters not only win a very prestig-ious award – sort of – but, more importantly, get the last and largest laugh …

It is simply not possible to keep bed-wetting a secret, at least not from your immediate family. Especially when it hits a person as often as it hits me.

How often? Well, it wasn't every blue moon, or every Friday the 13th, or even every pensioners' payday. It was much more regular than that.

How much more? Well, how can I phrase this deli-cately, and still come out looking like a lady?

I can't.

Alright, here's the truth, Ruth. I used to wet the bed every night. Sometimes twice a night. Thrice even. And I still do. Satisfied?

Me too.

So I have a problem with bladder control. Big deal. I reckon there'd be heaps worse things to have problems with. Like, what if you had a problem with temper con-trol, lost your rag real easy, and got into violent fights every day, punching people out and making enemies all over the park? That would suck.

And what if your problem was losing control of your mouth, and you couldn't help swearing horribly at people, and cussing out your teachers big-time. Then you'd get caned constantly, and be regarded as a foul-mouthed lowy.

Nobody hates me for wetting the bed. Nobody accuses me of publicly offending people. Bed-wetting is a very private thing. You only offend yourself. You only make an enemy of yourself, at least until you accept it as part of life and get on with your stuff.

So, this is a story about getting on with your stuff. This is a story about stuffing with your brother's stuff. This is a story about vengeance.

At last.

Let the record show that I admit, right from the start, that brother Rob is clever with one thing – money. He has it, he makes it, he chases it, he lusts after it. His whole life is dedicated to money, and using it to impress his richy-rich friends.

Rob the nob works in real-estate development. And he works hard at it, no doubt about that. He's got his own company, and turns over a couple of mill a year.

Big deal. It's always a big deal. Any time you ask Rob anything, the answer is always, 'Don't bother me now – I'm working on the details of a big deal.' Big deals – that's his whole life. He hasn't got time for people, except his snob-nob mates. For everyone else, even family, even if they've got a personal problem or need help, it's, 'Big deal – don't bother me.'

So it's surprising that the oldies would want to have anything to do with him. Oh sure, he's their only son and heir, and all that malarky, but deep down I suspect it comes back to that essentially evil ingredient that Rob the knob has in spades – money. Moolah. Dosh, sponduli, bread, hirays. Cash is king.

My oldies have a farm up in the valley. Our family has farmed the same area for three generations, but it was never very profitable. Farming is more a lifestyle than a way to make money.

That's why Rob made the momentous decision at eighteen to quit the farm, go to uni in the city, and study real estate.

He must have done alright, 'cause first year out of uni he'd bought, renovated, and sold for large profit three town houses. He got a taste for it then, and started buying old properties to demolish and build big ugly units on. He did this for a few years, cultivated a few dodgy contacts in the local council, got himself elected to the planning committee, and then went for it.

He went for it alright. Got the council to alter the zoning on all the local bush, and bought the lot. Then he lashed together a plan for a moneymaking venture so barefaced in its lust for profit that it would've shamed every flinty greedhead from the prime minister through to the local skag dealer.

When the local greenie groups got wind of Rob's plan to bulldoze the bush and create an insta-suburb on the denuded hills above town, they went berserk. They organised a big campaign that went national and got covered by the media coast to coast.

Rob and his cosy council cronies started getting cold feet. These greenies were putting up a good fight, and public opinion was swinging against the developers. Another week of that kind of negative media and they'd have no chance of getting their bulldozers within cooee of the bush. The greenies were already talking of setting up a bush blockade, and physically barring the bulldozers from entry.

Something had to be done. Time was of the essence. They had to act.

Crikey, you should've seen the response. The media went nuts. Everyone was horrified. Rob was more shunned than the dunny-cart man, and direct comparisons were made between Rob and the contents of the cart.

I agreed. What a turd. Rob didn't care about the rotten publicity – all he cared about was the development, and the profit. But *we* had to wear it too. We were his family, and we got tarred with the same brush. I got spat on at school, and called 'redneck'.

That wasn't fair. I wasn't the redneck – Rob was. His political leanings were a mixture of Attila the Hun, Joh Bonkers-Bananas, and Bozo the Clown. Rob hated greenies. The environment, in his view, was there to be built on. God only created trees to hold the ground together long enough for it to be concreted.

Rob saw nothing wrong in developers bulldozing old heritage houses in the dead of night, to get around zoning regulations and building laws and greenies. Joh

Bananas pulled it off in Brisbane, so why couldn't Rob do it in the bush?

Why not? Because it would be wrong.

But Rob did it anyway. He rallied the dozer drivers late at night and got the machinery in before the first greenie arrived. They worked hard, doing a full day's work in half a night. By morning the hill was cleared ...

Shocking stuff. I was ashamed to be his sister. Still am.

But we're getting off the track here. We were talking about my parents' farm, and Rob's involvement in it. Since they didn't make much out of it – money, that is – Rob the knob proposed a deal. He'd rent the big top paddock, which used to be a vineyard but had been let to go to seed. All the grape vines were overgrown, and the oldies didn't have the bucks to resurrect them.

So Rob jumped in. One of his devious city mates had put him onto a great tax dodge – vineyards. Rob hated paying tax. He reckoned he shouldn't have to. Dad said his attitude was outrageous and selfish. Everybody paid tax so we'd have schools and roads and hospitals and nursing homes. But Rob reckoned *nobody* should pay *any* tax, and everybody should pay for whatever services they need themselves. Which works just fine, as long as you're rich.

What about the elderly and frail? asked Dad. What about single mums and dads? What about people who can't afford high-priced medical care? What about the poor?

Bugger the poor, Rob thought to himself, but he didn't dare say it to Dad. After all, Mum and Dad were poor. Anyway, Rob hadn't come over to argue. He was here to make a deal, a big deal, that would cut his tax to nothing and earn the farm some much-needed revenue.

See, if Rob was able to invest his profits in the vineyard, he'd pay less tax, because his profits would become expenditure. If that sounds complicated, it was, which is why most normal people didn't do it. Working out those kind of finicky, tightwadded, mind-bendingly tedious details, just to get around paying tax, took an accountant with a brain the size of an earthmover and the morals of a hyaena.

Accountants like that certainly exist, and they cost a lot of money. Rob got one, and it cost a lot of money. But Rob had a lot of money. And, as he said, you have to spend money to make money. His accountant advised him to invest in the ramshackle vineyard.

The vineyard on our farm was sure *not* to make a profit because it was so small, and it had so much work to be done on it to bring it up to scratch, production-wise. And whatever money Rob spent on that would come out of Rob's tax. Instead of giving it to the taxman, Rob gave it to himself. Anyway, aside from writing off a major swedge of tax, Rob could make his own wine. Nothing impressed poshies and bignobs more than someone who owned a vineyard and made wine.

But, once again, we're getting way off the track. This was *my* story, and it was about bed-wetting, not Rob the knob's stay-rich schemes. But it does concern my oldies, so I guess that's where the tangent kicked in.

My parents are really cool. I mean that. Any normal

humans would have gone around the bend with my hard-core bed-wetting. Some nights Mum or Dad or both would get up three times to change my sheets. They got as little sleep as I did.

Yet, the whole time, they never roused on me. They never lost it, not once. They never tried to punish me for my perennial pissing performances. They only tried to help.

Their help was not always appreciated at the time. I got angrier with the whole caper than they did. Especially when they went out, without telling me, and brought home the buzz sheets.

Jeez. Buzz sheets? They were designed for old cotton-heads who couldn't feel their bodies any more, and couldn't tell the nurses that incontinence had once again transformed their warm nursing-home bed into a warm yellow lake.

Buzz sheets existed so nurses wouldn't have to reach into the bed themselves and feel around in disgust for wet patches. They were an electrified sheet, under another sheet of rubberised plastic, and every time the electrical current met with a urinal current, they went off.

Went off? Hell, in my case, they nearly blasted me out of bed. The alarm would start up – *whoop, whoop, whoop* – loud enough to wake the dead, and setting off all the hounds on neighbouring farms for miles around.

And if the alarm wasn't bad enough, the system had a light show to go with it. One whizz and my bedroom lit up like Christmas, with coloured light bulbs burning the darkness away like Roman candles and skyrockets on cracker night.

As soon as word got out what was causing the disco of light and sound that erupted from our farmhouse late each night, I became the local joke.

After three weeks of this hoax I insisted the oldies get rid of the anti-bed-wetting device, or I'd go and sleep in the old stone stables.

It was a good thing they didn't call my bluff, because the last place I wanted to sleep was the stables. I couldn't have got in there anyway. Rob kept the double doors padlocked. The stables had come with the vineyard, as part of the rental agreement, and Rob had decked them out with all his winemaking equipment.

The place stank of rotten grapes. Rob's early winemaking efforts had been very ordinary. Most of the wine went rotten in the bottles, and the clear green fluid went cloudy and weird. But after a few seasons Rob was getting decent grapes off the vines, and his wine started to improve. He upgraded his wine press, bought five new wooden barrels to ferment his overpriced grape juice, sixty unused wine bottles, and a machine to jam a cork in them.

And he started invited his dickwad friends around for wine-tasting nights. They were all super-rich (you had to be rich to be Rob's mate), and very snooty, and always brought bottles of wine produced by *their* vineyard. They had competitions to decide who produced the poshest plonk, and every year gave a poncy award for the best product.

It was September when Rob started organising another of his elitist wine-tasting parties. Only a dozen of the most important people were invited, and it was to be staged in October, in the stone stables. The stables had a chic, rustic air about them, and Rob planned to impress his pompous peers with a black-tie dinner, full silver service, waiters, doormen, the whole bit. Wanker.

I saw the invitations. No wonder Rob was going the whole hog. It was his turn to host the wine award ceremony. Everybody was to bring their finest plonk, and it would be judged that night by Rob the knob and his chintzy guests.

September was also the month that the oldies tried a whole new approach to combating my tremendous bedwetting capabilities. It was a complete shift in emphasis, a whole new approach, which Dad had read about when studying some medical journal, boning up on incontinence. There he read about a new system being trialled on chronic bed-wetters, which was basically the opposite of punishment.

My oldies had never punished me for bed-wetting, but some of their schemes to get me past the phase have certainly resulted in embarrassment and humiliation for me. So this new approach was a big step in the right direction.

The new method revolved around a reward system, and positive reinforcement. It worked like this; every time I got through a night without wetting the bed, I was given a silver star. Three silver stars and I earned a gold star. Three gold stars and I received a gift of my choice to the value of fifty bucks.

Now *here* was a glimmer of hope. Here was a chance

to win presents. And all I had to do was keep the bed dry. Easy.

Well, easier said than done. But not impossible.

Every night when I crashed I hit the sack wearing pilchers. Yes, you heard right – pilchers. Yes, OK, plastic baby pants. I've worn them all my life. Get over it.

Every morning my Mum would check my pilchers. And every morning, at least until they tried the reward system, my pilchers were sopping wet, bloated out like a spacesuit with all the wee sloshing around inside them.

But when the oldies shifted to the silver and gold stars, my behavioural patterns shifted too. Suddenly Mum was finding bone-dry pilchers – day after day. My parents were stoked. They got sleep. They celebrated with me when I got my first silver star, my first gold, my first fifty-dollar present, my second, my third …

They couldn't believe the change. At last. They wouldn't have to worry any more about having a teenage daughter wetting the bed. Their worries dried up overnight, if you'll excuse the expression.

But then I started feeling guilty. They were too poor to keep buying me presents, and especially presents I hadn't rightfully earned.

Yep, I was cheating. What else could I do? I've told you once – I'm chronic. I can't stop wetting the bed. All my dreams end with me squatting on a toilet, at which point I go, and and so does the dream. I wake up in a puddle. There was no way to stem the flow, as it were, and definitely no way stop it, stars or no stars.

Can I just say in my defence that half the reason I

cheated was so Mum and Dad would get some peace of mind. They were more het up over it than I was. So I slipped into the local supermarket and bought a big bag of pilchers, which I secreted in my bedroom. Every night when the dream took me to the toilet, I'd wake, stick a hose into the reservoir of wee that filled my elasticated plastic pants, and drain it off into a twenty-litre drum I kept hidden under my bed.

Then I'd get a fresh pair of pilchers from my stash, chuck them on, and crash.

I got tired of feeling low and sneaky every morning, when I'd wake to dry pants, and claps and cheers from the oldies. Only Rob the knob sneered, whenever he was around to see the performance.

And he was around a lot, especially in October. He spent three weeks working on the stables and in the vineyard to ensure his wine-tasting party scene was heaps special. He rigged out a mondo-expenso sound system and techo lights that were radar controlled and operated by remote.

Soon everything was in place for the big night. Rob had spent the last weeks before the party bottling his wine from the wooden barrels. It was last year's vintage, a very special drop that he'd been experimenting with, and the two dozen bottles he ended up with had cost him a fortune. He was secretly confident of taking out the award for this year's best – you could tell by the conceited smile that grew across his dial like a rash every time he held a bottle of his yellow gold up to the sun and thanked God for making him so clever and talented. Tool.

The big night finally arrived, and Rob paced the stone stables, nervous with anticipation. He polished the twenty-four bottles of boutique wine he'd produced, fondling each one like a gold ingot. He straightened a fork at a place-setting on the table. He had that feeling in the pit of his stomach again – the feeling he got that night he bulldozed the bush. He now knew it to be the feeling that preceded great victories. Would it be tonight? Was that it? He knew it was. And he knew what it meant – the wine award. Sure as.

The soiree kicked off in high style, with waiters bearing champagne and nibblies, and an elegant string band playing angelic music. The guests arrived by chauffeured limo by ones and twos – you didn't arrive crammed into a limo with others, not if you wanted to make an impression. No, you travelled alone and arrived properly if you desired a suitably grand entrance. Leave car-pooling to the plebs.

Everyone chatted importantly for a stretch, and the dinner gong rang. I had hidden myself up in the loft hours before, so I could observe the whole decadent scene. It was uncomfortable up there with the itchy hay and rats running across the rafters, but the view was superb.

Rob had hired the city's top caterers, so the food was top notch, obviously, and each guest in turn produced a few bottles of their own home-grown plonk, to be drunk over dinner. They argued and ribbed each other over who would snatch their grand winemaking award. Although it wasn't worth anything as such, it carried maximum prestige, much kudos, and would be talked about in all the right places. Everyone wanted that award.

Finally dinner was finished, and the waiters cleared up. Rob stood at the head of the long table, with five bottles of his wine, uncorked half an hour before to 'let it breathe'.

Now he passed the bottles along the table, poured some wine into his own glass, and proposed a toast. The guests couldn't agree on whether the toast should be to the Queen, the Republic, or themselves. Finally they settled on 'Greed is Good'.

Rob and his richy-snitch mates took a deep sniff of the vineyard's special experiment wine. There was silence around the table. Rob looked perplexed, and took another sniff of his glass.

'Good nose on it, Robert, old chap,' muttered Siimeon Wrenbrane, who had a pretty good one on himself. He was an advertising industry tar baby, the biggest wanker west of Casablanca, but he was rich, so Rob had invited him.

There were grunts of agreement around the spotless table. 'Yes, good nose, fine aroma, what! Let's have a look at it then, shall we, what!'

They did. Around the table every wrist was raised, and the colour, viscosity, and overall visual appeal of the contents were summed up in one word from Siimeon: 'Exquisite! Now for the real test.' He raised the glass to his lips.

The others joined him, their delicate mouths poised for what they knew would be something akin to the nectar of the gods. Robert had spent *so* much money on it – it had to be good.

The guests took fairy sips of the sparkling yellow wine. Their tastebuds couldn't get a grip on the obscure flavour, so they followed the sip with a deeper draught.

'Delicate flavours, Robert. Reminds me of clover in summer,' snuffled Amanda O'Cheap, the acidic wine critic who penned the muckrake 'Whine and Die' column in *The Sourier-Grape*.

'Quite lovely – one of the season's finest,' she added.

'Yes, I agree, completely. But don't go misquoting me on that Amanda, just to get a story, like those other poor saps you interview.' That rude but justifiable comment came from Dorian Rhinobottom, whose family were from old money, the Rhinobottoms of Hackneyed Common. Dorian thought Rob's vino the best drop he'd guzzled all year. He slurped off the remains of his glass, then downed a second, and a third.

Penelope Sloane was of the opinion that it compared most favourably with the famous Chatterly '78, from the upper Plonker Valley.

Maybe she had a point.

Pamela Wilson-Wallflower, another journo, wrote articles for the weekend screamer *The Sunday Terror*. In that capacity she arrived at Rob's do already sloshed, and raving. Everything was 'boorish' to her. Her boss was boorish. Her boyfriend was 'boorish'. Kids' books were boorish. In reality, *she* was boorish. Now she drunkenly added her two bob's worth: 'A great guzzle, Robert – far from boorish.'

'Yes' said Alistair Allbutt. 'This is definitely the high point of the year in wine, for me.'

For me too, Allbutt.

'Yes, I think we're all agreed,' announced Melanie Backward. 'Your wine is ab fab, Robert — fine enough to drink at Kirribilli House. I must ask Daddy to stock the cellar with it. And that label is as cute as my little red MG.'

All eyes went to the label, including Rob the knob's. Uh oh.

There were titters around the table, and polite snuffles. 'What a frightfully witty joke,' someone commented. Only Rob said nothing. He stared at the label. It wasn't the label he'd stuck on. It was the oval sticker off the pilchers packets, the brand of pilchers I wore, with a picture of a baby looking dry and comfortable in her cheap plastic duds.

The blood drained from Rob's face. He jerked his reading glasses out of his jacket pocket and jammed them onto his face. Then he read the name of the wine he'd just served his esteemed guests — Vin du Urine.

'Yes, it must be jolly well unanimous then,' said Siimeon. 'I say Robert's rare wine wins this year's trophy hands down. All in favour say "aye". That's it then. The ayes have it. Congratulations, Robert. A fine drop. You must be very proud of yourself.'

Himself? *Himself?* What about *me*?

Rob the knob got up then and made some cheap thank-you speech, but he couldn't get it together. He was stammering, and shaking, and sweating like a gorgon with plague.

His guests smiled. They were having a jolly nice time, eating important food and drinking important wine with important people, just like them. They sipped more of Rob's wine, and nodded their heads. Good drop. Yes, jolly good drop. Rob nodded, his face as white as a morgue wall, but he wouldn't sip any more of his prize-winning wine.

It reminded me of a scene from *The Emperor's New Clothes*.

You could see the idea working over in Rob's guests' heads. 'I know it's good wine, because Robert's been experimenting with some new and unusual grapes, plus he has all the latest technology. Therefore the wine must be superb. Everyone else has raved about it, so I'd better too, or I'll look like an ignorant fool. It *must* be good, but, well, in that case, why does it taste so much like … piss?'

Maybe I forget to tell you that I'd always known where Rob hid the keys to the stable. And I'm certain I forgot to tell you about all those times I'd poured Rob's wine down the drain and refilled the bottles, siphoning the contents from my secret wee drum under the bed. How else was I going to get gold stars off the oldies? How else was I going to win stuff? And how else was I going to get rid of that much wee?

It was the only way. I bottled my vin de urine, and Rob's mates drank it – then gave him an award for it. How unfair. That was *my* product. It should've been *my* award. But then again, I think I got rewarded enough …

---

*Special thanks to Marnie Dixon for planting the seeds of this story.*

# Locker 13

Alright. Wez was prepared to admit he'd been pretty bad on one or two or maybe a few occasions. Yes, OK, majorly bad. Feral. But that was all in the past now – give a kid a break – and Wez swore to anyone who'd listen that he'd turned over a new leaf. Really.

Wez had turned the leaf over in the schoolyard when he'd been doing scab duty. He'd spied a frog lurking under it, and stomped the stray hopper to a grisly green paste. The principal had seen what happened and chucked a serious wobbly. He was a nature lover, and expelled Wez on the spot, for treading on frogs.

Everyone thought that was fair, except Wez.

Expelled again. Wez was hurt (he thought it a pretty trivial offence), the frog was hurt (newsflash: the frog was RS), and the principal was hurt (that he had to do it). Or so he said, though he smiled when he said that bit.

Anyway, the principal was not one to dwell on the negative. He told Wez to look on the bright side – the boy had just busted the record for the state's most expelled student.

Wez was the new state school-expulsion champion!

Well. Most kids don't win a state *anything*. Wez was stoked, and proud, and suitably strutty. Now his name would be in the most prestigious history book of the lot – the state schools' Big Black Book. He'd be a significant statistic. He'd be admired. He'd be famous. He'd be mobbed by paparazzi.

But – predictably – there was a catch.

With Wez now ranked as the worst kid in the state, no normal school would enrol him. He'd gone through the lot, nearly, and the bigwig education authorities had run out of ideas. They didn't know what to do with him. He was far too bad for prison, and way too smart for Maccas.

Wez just wanted to stay a schoolkid, get a good education, and one day become a ruthless corporate high-flier, but he was too poor to study interstate or overseas. Wez had run out of options. He'd blown it.

Or nearly blown it. There was one chance. There was one school in the state that would take Wez. The one school in the state that had *no* standards. A school that wasn't picky. A school that wasn't choosy. A school that would register a werewolf, no questions asked, provided it rolled up in uniform three days out of five, and didn't hang around the canteen door begging meat scraps.

There was only one school where Wez's sort of caper was considered normal, acceptable, even ordinary – Peculiar High.

The only school in the state that would enrol Wez was Peculiar High. That thought caught him in the stomach like a punch. He'd heard total crims talk about the school, in hushed whispers and quavering tones, but Wez had never imagined he'd have to *go* there. He never guessed he'd sink so low …

Some kids talk about their school being like a gaol, but Peculiar High *was* a gaol. At least the island, and the buildings, and high bluestone walls surrounding it *used* to be a gaol. It was a real Devil's Island-type joint – stark, menacing stone walls built on a jagged, rocky volcanic plug that rose out of the harbour.

The place was mega gothic, and mega unpleasant. The gaol routine itself had been a living nightmare. The prison officers were meaner than measles, the food was cold slop rejected by the local piggery on health grounds, and the televisions only got Channel Nine.

In fact, the gaol was such a savage deterrent that it was forced to close – its reputation was so crook the entire area became law-abiding overnight, and simply ran out of criminals. Suddenly there was no more profit to be made out of the bad-guy business.

The whole place went broke and shut down, and there were mass sackings. All the mean prison officers lost their jobs, and the ex-cons cheered, which, if nothing else, goes to show the importance of being pleasant to your customers – if you're in that line of work …

After the gaol closed, Peculiar High took over the island. The school never actually bought the prison buildings, or officially opened, or even got a license. Like weed seed, it just invaded the place, a cloud of toxic spores blown across the water and into the cracks and ditches and belfry of the solemn, creepy stone joint.

The weird high school grew, and festered, and spread, like a putrid tropical ulcer with a side serve of maggots. Soon it harboured hundreds of hardened 'pupils', who, like Wez, had nowhere else to go. That was just the official numbers. Unofficially the rabid mongrel swarm was sometimes in the thousands, but it was hard to headcount when dozens seemed to arrive every week, while dozens more disappeared.

Peculiar High's rep spread like a sickening strain of Spanish flu in a seriously Spanish area of Spain. Only the baddest of the bad went there, they never lasted, and they were, generally speaking, never seen again …

Now Wez was going there.

Being the new kid in school sucks, on many levels. At Peculiar High it sucked on every level. Wez was introduced to the whole school in one hit by Principal Fleeburn, right up on assembly, and pelted with stale sandwiches and rotten fruit and putrid eggs for the next four minutes.

He met his teachers, six in all. Three came right out and asked for a loan of money, any amount, small change even. The maths teacher brazenly blackmailed him – 'fifty bucks by Tuesday or you're cactus in calculus' – and when Wez met the last two they didn't even get a chance to chat. They were busy people, no time to talk, especially when one was chasing the other, swinging a gleaming hatchet, screaming something about blood, and murder, and stolen racing pigeons.

Wez stepped out for a breath of fresh air to get his head together, but everywhere he went was just as bizarre. Near the entrance of the school was a set of splintery old stocks, the kind that convicts were forced to squat at with their wrists and ankles manacled. Anywhere else they'd have been left *in situ* as a quaint and colourful reminder of Australia's cruel convict past, but at Peculiar High they were still in use, twenty-four hours a day, in high rotation. Wez, being the decent dude that he was, tried to slip the poor shrivelled prisoner a sip of water, but had to run off when a teacher threatened to collar him there instead.

At the the highest point of the stone island was a gallows which, thankfully, didn't have anybody hanging from it. But when Wez asked someone why it was still there, he was cheerfully informed that six students had been stretched just last week – four for smiling, and two for whistling. And when Wez went up to have a closer look at the hanging platform, he found, to his horror, a rusty old metal gibbet dangling from a tree, with three chalky stiffs skeletonising in it.

Wez was shocked, but that was nothing for Peculiar High. Stranger things were coming …

It was Peculiar High tradition that the new kid go through a period of 'initiation'. Like in any solid democratic institution, Wez had choices – three. Swim fully clothed in the school dam. Wear the school sack over his head for three weeks. Or move all his stuff into Locker 13.

Wez chose Locker 13. It was probably a smart choice. He'd seen the school dam. Half a bloated dead cow on one bank, a litter of schoolbags, shoes and torn clothes on another, and, massing in the centre, half a dozen dorsal fins belonging to what Wez could only describe as very, *very* large sharks.

He had seen the head sack, too. A normal enough piece of farmyard haberdashery, nice hessian cloth, good quality, well stitched … then dunked daily in the school sewage and seasoned with a beaker of elephant lice. *Prêt-à-porter*, ready to wear, every day for three weeks.

Wez could see which way the wind blew, and chose Locker 13. It was well and truly out of the wind. And light. Hardly any oxygen, either. Right up the end of the bag hall, and a sharp left into the cellar. Down some stone steps, along a bit, left, right, right, right, or was that left? Wherever. The directions aren't important, because there, down in the dark, musty, dripping cavity, stood Locker 13.

Wez nervously cleared his throat, and clenched his fists. He knew whatever was in Locker 13 was bad. Bad? Hell, it had to be murderous to match the other initiation choices. But, murderous or not, Wez had to use the locker. If he didn't, he'd fail initiation and get kicked out of school – forever. Plus it was the only spare locker. Wez wasn't pleased, but he knew he had to secure his stuff. The joint was probably crawling with thieves.

He stepped up to Locker 13. Sprayed across its steel door were rusty bullet holes, with thick tufts of wiry spider web bristling out of them, like hair sprouting out of an old bloke's earholes. The big, darting funnel–web spiders that had spun the web chased each other through the jagged axe–attack holes in the side of the locker.

A fine spray of what looked suspiciously like fresh-ish human blood had coagulated across the rusty locker door, partly obscuring the sinister symbols scorched on with a blowtorch flame. Wez scraped some flaky blood off to reveal a skull and crossbones, and the number 13.

A long, thick, crispy snakeskin ran twice around the locker's base like a satanic scarf, and a gruesome clutch of yellowing human teeth on a leather strap formed its demonic necklace.

It was sick. It was twisted. It was wrong. But it *was* a locker – and it locked and all. Wez gripped the key in his shaking fingers. He drew a breath, and held it in, then let it out. He scraped some dried guts off the keyhole with his thumbnail, and inserted the key. He gently turned it.

The tumblers clicked. Wez turned the handle. He pulled. With a spooky, groaning creak the door lurched open.

There it was. The inside of Locker 13. His locker.

Cool, thought Wez. The locker was empty, except for the spiders. It was sturdy. It was roomy. It had two levels. It was everything a bloke looked for in a locker, with the added advantage of privacy. Wez was jazzed. He liked how mad Locker 13 looked. He would've decked it out that way himself, and his favourite animals were spiders.

But Wez was in school, not some discussion panel talking locker fashions, so pretty soon he knuckled down to his study. Workwise he was leagues ahead in his classes – nobody else turned up. Not even the teachers.

Most of the students hung out in the quadrangle, swinging from the light poles, or hooked upside down from the trees like hoodlum orang-outangs, toking on cigarettes held in their bare toes. Teachers lolled around in the shade, drinking bootleg beer, betting on cards, and cursing Creation and all its lowly manifestations.

The principal herself wandered the decks like the town dero, singing filthy sailor songs and reciting bawdy cathouse doggerel, pausing mid-stanza to light a student's cigar, or compare their latest tattoos.

It was at that point Wez realised if he was going to get educated he had to do it himself …

That woz eezier sed than dun – Wez couldn't even spell rite. And where do you start in getting an education when you've always treated school as a great, big, hairy practical joke? Wez figured the answer to his questions probably lay somewhere in schoolbooks, and went to borrow a whole whack of them from the library.

The librarian was asleep in a rocking chair near the front desk. He had cobwebs growing across his head and smelled vaguely of mange, or month-old compost scraps, or a dead thing. He looked like Frankenstein while he slept, and Godzilla when Wez suddenly woke him.

After a lot of muttering and mumbling and veiled threats of violence the weirdo librarian let Wez through. The books housed within the dark building looked like they hadn't been picked up in years, smothered in dust and half mauled by earwigs and book bugs. But Wez found a few that looked interesting, and took them to the front desk.

Wez had nearly finished filling out the borrower's card, and just written '13' in the space requesting the borrower's locker number, when the freak librarian read the entry upside down. Locker 13! He went white. He suddenly started ranting madly about demons, and devils, and Satan's slaves, and all the Powers of Darkness! Then he ran screaming from the building like a rat in a firestorm.

Wez shrugged it off and took the books anyway. He stashed them carefully in his locker, and sloped off to eat his lunch alone under a tree on the tiny exercise oval.

Wez ate a leisurely lunch, and opened the locker an hour later to retrieve the books. A foul smell instantly assaulted his nostrils. Spattered right across the books was a pile of steaming, squirming, slimy, stinking entrails.

Wez was spun. The locker had been locked, the obvious thing to do with lockers. Who *else* had a key? And what did they mean by dropping their guts in there?

Wez figured the filthy gift was a one-off from some sick unit, and it wouldn't happen again. He cleaned it out and got on with his doings. But next day he opened his locker and found a sheep's brain slopped on two textbooks on the top shelf. Whoever had done it had only just done it – the brain was fresh. Fresh? The filthy thing was still pulsating, and Wez had to stab the slimy pink ball repeatedly with his green pen to stop it rolling around on his stuff.

Wez decided a casual approach was his best chance of catching the demented locker invader. Play the waiting game – pretend nothing had happened, go about his business, then, when no-one was looking, hook a four-forty-volt electrical wire up to the inside of the locker door. Next person who touched it – *whoompa!* – shock city. Then just hunt down the wild-eyed kid with smoke seeping out his ears and the instant Don King haircut, and he'd have the culprit nailed worse than Jesus.

Wez duly installed the bodacious booby-trap on the sly. Nobody saw him do it. The dangerous device contained a tiny light bulb, to switch on when the trap was triggered.

Next day Wez checked the light bulb – it was still off. No-one had touched it. Wez deactivated the deadly electrical hook-up and casually opened the locker door, to reveal a very gruesome tableau. A cow's head, freshly removed, dripping blood, eyes bugged, tongue lolling, lifelessly squatted on the shelf. Wez nearly gagged with disgust as he removed the unholy item, and vowed he'd fix whoever was persecuting him with the filthy cuts of meat.

Wez knew his nemesis was probably some criminal genius, hired by the school to make his time hell. Whoever it was, they were pros, and obviously capable of avoiding Wez's electric burglar stopper. Wez had to go high-techo.

He rigged a small video camera and a long-playing tape just above Locker 13, camouflaged it with moss and slime, and set it on slow-record. Once he'd recorded the low-life offender on camera, it would just be a matter of time before he'd track them down. Then he'd unleash a hell broth of revenge, massive reprisals, a veritable reign of terror! Plus he'd make them mop the meat stink out of Locker 13, which was started to smell like a dingy butcher's shop.

Wez set the camera recording and left. Next day, when he opened his locker, what did he find? Four fresh, athletic-looking pig's trotters, impaled on spikes, mid-stride, jogging in midair.

Right – this was it! The camera never lied. Now he'd bust this bodgie bandit.

Wez trawled through the video footage, hours of it, and couldn't believe what he saw –there was absolutely nothing on the tape. Nothing. The only human he saw on the video tape was himself. Nobody had been near Locker 13, except Wez.

Impossible.

Then Wez figured maybe he'd been too sophisticated in his entrapment procedures. Maybe what he needed was a cruder, more hands-on approach. He set a bunch of steel rabbit traps on both levels of the locker.

Naturally enough, when he returned next day, he found fresh rabbits in each of them. Only these rabbits had been skinned, and gutted, and rubbed with aromatic herbs, all ready to cook up into some classy culinary concoction.

This was getting very weird.

There was a definite pattern emerging, but Wez was too flummoxed to pick up on it. Not when the pot roast appeared from thin air. Not when he found a half kilo of prime Scotch fillet on the top shelf. Not even the bag of osso buco twigged his wig. Two dozen pork sausages. Lamb chump chops, trimmed of fat, at least half a kilo. A great wedge of lean roo rump, restaurant quality, top shelf, hard to get these days unless you know someone …

Wez still didn't get it.

Then he found the generous meat tray, and the short, terse note written in meat juice on a ragged scrap of bloodied butcher's paper. 'U.O.I.4.'

What in the hell did that mean? Who owed whom four? And four what? And what for?

Wez was baffled, obviously, but intrigued. Whoever was plaguing him with manky meat products must have written the note. It was the first and only contact Wez had received from them. It must, therefore, hold solid clues as to their identity. But there was nothing in it to provide a clue. No names. No dates. And it made no sense.

There wasn't a lot about Locker 13 that *did* make sense. Its very existence in the bowels of Peculiar High was a story too obscure and strange and creepy to even begin to relate to a decent, normal reader.

So here we go:

Locker 13 had been the silent sentinel in the slimy cellar for longer than anyone could remember. It had been there long before Peculiar High mutated on the island, and none of the gaol records made any reference to it being ordered or delivered. The gaol had had no knowledge of it, because nobody they knew had delivered it.

Back in the dying days of the nineteenth century, around the time the hulking stone prison was being built by convicts on the craggy volcanic plug in the harbour, a bunch of kids worked as apprentices to a local butcher.

They all had their own knives and butchery tools, and each kept them sharp and polished, just like the boss ordered. And they kept them locked away, securely, in their individual lockers in the apprentices' shed and tea room.

There was one apprentice, called Claude, who suffered epileptic fits sometimes. Very little – make that nothing –

was known about epilepsy or epileptic fits back then, and most people thought Claude was mad as a fruit bat. The butcher was a good bloke and kept the weedy Claude on because of his superior skills, but even he got embarrassed when Claude took a fit and had to be restrained by half a dozen kids, again and again.

One day – a Wednesday as it happened – the other apprentices trapped Claude in the coldroom and locked him in his locker. The poor kid beat on the door and screamed and made a hellish racket that only the apprentices heard – the butcher was away at the Butchers' Picnic.

Trapped in the locker like a rat in a bottle, Claude freaked out and fitted repeatedly. When the apprentices opened the door again, ten or fifteen minutes later, he was dead.

Think of the worst trouble you've known, then triple it – then triple that. This was big-brand trouble. This was murder. This was late nineteenth century, and murder meant the death penalty. The death penalty meant hanging by the neck …

Heavy.

What could they do? What would you do? The other terrified apprentices panicked big-time, bundled the body back into the locker, and locked it.

That night they broke into the shed, carried the locker to a nearby rowboat, and set off, shivering with cold, and fear, and horror.

When the rowers neared the half-built stone gaol, in the deepest part of the harbour, they opened the locker and jettisoned Claude's cold cadaver overboard. There was a slap, a quiet gurgle, then a long, spooky sigh, as the body slowly sank into the dark waters.

The harbour was infested with sharks, so that was the body taken care of. Now they just had to unload Claude's cursed coffin, the locker. They lugged it ashore at the gaol site, carrying it down deep into the dark dungeons and tunnels of the building. Exhausted, they dumped the locker in a musty corner and fled.

They were never caught, and not much was really made of Claude's disappearance. He'd been regarded by everyone as terminally nutso, and disappearing was regarded as a typically terminally nutso thing to do. Everyone accepted that as a good explanation and got on with their thing, but those apprentice kids carried their terrible secret all their long sorrowful lives, to their lonely, silent graves.

If they'd been caught they'd have swung from the gallows on the very island Claude's lonely locker lurked. They sweated like hell when they realised they themselves were finally dying. They made deathbed confessions, but that was too late – they'd had a lifetime of punishment already.

Claude's locker, the dark, cursed cocoon where he'd died in a frenzied fit, was now Wez's locker. Locker 13. And, if Wez was going to use Claude's locker, then he'd better damned well give Claude what he was owed ...

'U.O.I.4.' – Wez read the note again, then read it backwards, then held it over a flame to see if anything else was written invisibly in lemon juice. He'd read all about that sort of deep-cover bizzo in a spicy spy story, and hoped to read something amazing and profound as the invisible ink warmed up. But the note just caught fire, went up like a sailor's distress flare, and scorched all the hairs in Wez's nostrils.

He danced around in agony, lungs full of the charred stink of his own burnt nose-hair, and he would've kept cursing and swearing and carrying on for a good deal longer if he hadn't heard the laughter.

He stopped and peered around. There was nobody beside him. There was nobody behind him. And there was the laugh again – coming from the locker ...

Wez stepped back, then forwards, then back again, unsure what to do next. Gingerly he opened the locker, almost against his will. He was scared. Scared? He was packing it!

Crouched in the lower section of the locker, wet and bedraggled like a drowned dog, and pale as ivory, was the flickering grey ghost of Claude, the butcher's apprentice.

'You owe me four days',' the ghost croaked. It picked some seaweed from between its spectral teeth with a grimy fingernail, and glared at Wez.

'What?' sputtered Wez.

'You owe me four days'.'

'What?' repeated Wez, stonkered to stone. 'Four days' what?'

'Four days' pay, yer dodo. Thursday was pay day and I died on Wednesday, and I didn't get me pay. You owe me four days. So pay up.'

Wez rubbed his eyes and pummelled his ears and scratched his goolies, but the apparition was still there. This obviously wasn't a dream. He cleared his throat nervously.

'Look, I don't know who or what you are, or what in the hell you're talking about, but if it's you who keeps leaving that sick stuff in my locker, then stop it.'

'Course it's me, ya dense cove. How else am I gunna get me pay?'

'I don't know anything about any pay. Just rack off, right?'

'Rack off? Rack off lamb, maybe? Or a nice rack off ribs? I can do both. Nice cuts, too; nice enough for yer grey-haired granny's Sundy tea with the vicar – I do 'em real nice. I nearly got me ticket you know.'

'Ticket? Ticket to where?'

'Ticket to be a butcher, ya dunderhead. And I would've been a real good one too. I *was* a real good one. So I want me wages. Now!'

'Why should I pay you your wages?'

'Because you've got me locker, that's why. Who else can I get it off? They're all dead now. Bastards. They owe me four shillings.'

'Four *shillings*? Look mate, even if I wanted to pay your wages I couldn't. We don't have that old money any more.'

'That doesn't matter – I'll accept any currency. Doubloons, pieces of eight, gold dollars …'

'Gold dollars? How many gold dollars is four shillings.'

'How in the hell would I know? Look it up in yer fancy-pants learning books.'

So Wez did. And he found the answer straight away, in the tables conversion section of a maths book. Four shillings was eighty cents, equivalent.

'Eighty cents?' snorted Wez derisively. 'I got paid more

pocket money when I was five. Eighty cents! You've been skinned.'

'Skins? Sausage skins? Stomach skin, straight from a fresh cow's guts, make a lovely piece of tripe fer yer supper, or maybe …'

'Look. If I pay your four days' wages will you leave me alone, and stop dumping shitey lumps of dead meat in my locker?'

'Certainly.'

'Right. Here's a gold dollar. That's five days' wages.'

'But I don't have any change.'

'Forget it. Twenty cents is nothing.'

'But I didn't earn it. I can't just take it. It wouldn't be right.'

'Forget it. It's a bonus – for the Afterlife.'

'Alright, but I have to do something in return. Anyone you want filleted?'

'What do you mean "filleted"?'

'Fixed. Spooked. Scared stupid. Destroyed.'

'Yeah, like only the whole place …'

'Easily done. You want the whole place destroyed? Follow me.'

Like smoke the ghost drifted into the back of the locker, and then through it. Wez could follow – a concealed tunnel was burrowed through the wall behind the locker, hidden by a dark flimsy screen. Wez got down into the locker, and went through the back, crawling and squirming as best he could to keep up with the ectoplasmic apprentice that floated before him.

Finally, after Wez had crawled for what felt like miles,

the ghost slipped into a cavernous opening, and stopped. It was dark in the cave, but Claude emanated a soft white light. By the ghost's thin illumination Wez could just see the floor of the cavern. Set solidly into the stone foundations was a big stone thingy that looked a lot like a large plughole. Stoppered in it was another big stone thingy that looked very much like a large plug.

'What's that?' asked Wez, gasping to catch his breath.

'What does it look like?'

'I dunno. A big stone plug?'

'Exactly. This whole place is built on a volcanic plug. And there it is.'

'Bullshit! A volcanic plug is just a bit of rock left over when a volcano goes off. You're a moron. *That's* not a volcanic plug.'

'Oh yeah, wise guy? Well why don't you pull it out then?'

'OK. I will.'


Wez was lucky to get away with his life. As it was all his clothes were completely burnt off in the blasting gush of volcanic lava, and his head was singed bald.

Luckily he was blown ahead of the lava, some fair distance out to sea, stark naked and well shocked. From his vantage point treading water in the middle of the harbour – actually the *exact* spot Claude was dumped a hundred years before – he watched Peculiar High, and its weirdo inhabitants, burn and frizzle and jiggle and fry like ants on a barbecue. Then the place just went off, blew itself skyward with an immense explosion, and sank into the depths of the bay.

There were scarcely enough pieces left for the ghoulish souvenir hunters …

Years later, when Wez was a ruthless corporate high-flier, he'd swear to anyone who'd listen that educating himself was the best thing he ever did with his life. That, and paying a ghost its long-overdue wages – plus a small bonus for the Afterlife …

# Bludge Tuesday

**B** arry Roughead left school at the first possible opportunity, the exact instant he turned twelve and nine months. He'd been born at three minutes past midday, so that moment occurred smack in the middle of double maths.

Barry checked his watch, abruptly stood, gave the maths teacher the bird, and loudly mocked the rest of his class for being rat-brained goody-goodies. Then he strode out of the class room, out the front gate, and off the school grounds, into a bright and glorious future.

'Right,' Barry muttered to himself. 'That's that. Free at last. What am I going to do now?'

He was genuinely surprised that nobody had pounced on him the second he stepped off the school grounds, with some grouse job offer. He was, after all, eminently employable. He was as sharp as a razor, smarter than a cyborg, and knew more about life than all the presidents and prime ministers of the world put together. He was also a fine-looking chap, according to his granny, had a ripper set of muscles, a sick haircut, twenty-twenty vision, and all his own teeth.

Yet, remarkably, this wasn't enough. Nobody outside the school gate approached him with the offer of a high-paid job. They didn't head-hunt him on the way home. They hadn't caught up with him by the time he got to the front door of his house, either.

'Where are they?' Barry asked himself, genuinely stonk-ered. How could they have overlooked him? How could any self-respecting company get by without the priceless services of Barry Roughead?

Barry sat at home for a month, unemployed, watching the midday 'Mundane Show' on the idiot box, and rubbing his chin in deep perplexity.

'You need a haircut and a proper job,' Barry's dad, Larry Roughead, stated. 'The problem with the youth of today is they don't know the meaning of a hard day's work. Plus they wear all that metal in their faces. Plus they all carry butterfly knives in their back pockets. Pauline Hateson's right, you know. All you kids should be made to go in the army, and carry guns instead of knives. How are you supposed to kill boat-people with a bloody knife? Plus they should send all the Aborigines back overseas where they came from.'

It was a Tuesday, and Larry Roughead was slacking around at home, taking a sickie. He wasn't sick at all, but as Mr Roughead always said, 'What's the use of taking a sickie when you're sick – might as well be miserable at work.'

Larry Roughead suddenly caught a fine idea, from his redneck dad. Every Tuesday his dad took a sickie. So did all the other workers in his street. And all the workers in his suburb. All the workers in the country did it, in fact. Just about everyone who had a job took Tuesday sickies. That's where Barry Roughead first got his gold-plated business idea, the one sure to make him a millionaire by thirteen.

It was time to act.


Sickies were first invented by an office drone called Sonya Barking-Mad, who figured her hairbrained boss would never cotton on to the fact that it was acute slackness – rather than illness – that made her take every Monday and Friday off work, supposedly sick.

To facilitate her four-day weekends Sonya Barking-Mad would ring in with progressively more outlandish excuses. She started with the obvious ones – a twisted eye, a sprained ear, an infected hairpiece.

But soon she'd run out of the garden-variety maladies, and resorted to severe more and more bizarre diseases – typhoid, cerebral malaria, deadly dropsy, and killer Spanish flu. Galloping gangrene made an appearance, measles and poliomyelitis were regular afflictions, and fatal bouts of beri-beri began to badger her on a fortnightly basis.

Sonya's boss pretty soon realised he had an incurable sloth on his hands, and put the kybosh on her sickies. He gave her the boot and sent her packing with a sacking. Sonya was genuinely surprised that her crapola excuses weren't believed.

But this is not Sonya's story, or, if it was, it isn't any more. After Sonya Barking-Mad invented the sickie, Australian workers took to it with a vengeance. Every Aussie wanted a piece of that ripper idea, and starting taking Mondays and Fridays off work whenever the mood gripped them. Jobs became a joke. The work just wasn't being done any more. Business suffered. Something had to change.

The government put their Minister for Hard Work, Peter Third-Reich, onto the job. He made it illegal, punishable by imprisonment and flogging, for any worker to take Friday or Monday sickies. Bad luck if they *were* genuinely sick – they could die on the production line for all Mr Third-Reich cared.

That was that taken care of.

But the minister wasn't smart enough by half. Workers started getting around the law by taking *Tuesdays* off.

Tuesday had always been a crap day. On Monday, workers were still in shock at the fact that their weekend was over and they were back to the grind, but by Tuesday the ugly reality had really sunk in – the week had just started.

So Tuesday became the obvious day to take a sickie, and all the workers jumped on the bandwagon. Bludge Tuesday became the single most dangerous threat to Australian industry, an ugly syndrome that looked set to grind a once proud country into the dust.

Which is where this story finally becomes Barry Roughead's story again. About bloody time.

Remember Barry? Disillusioned unemployed teenager, no-hoper heading-straight-for-the-dole-queues, acne-faced loser boy. Well not for long. See Barry, in a burst of pure inspiration, suddenly came up with a mad, rad, fully bad idea how to make money out of someone else's misery.

He decided to start an employment company to fill the Bludge Tuesday sickie lists, when half the nation's workforce was at home on the bludge.

It was an uncharacteristically fantabulous idea for a dingbat like Barry – a real corker. It was sure to succeed. After all, just about every business in the country needed people to work on Tuesdays, to cover for the workers who were skiving off at home. There were heaps of jobs vacant. Barry could have first choice of all the prime jobs, and charge a blimmin' fortune.

Which he did.

Barry Roughead's employment company, which he called Bludge Tuesday Employment, was an overnight success. The phones ran hot day and night. Businesses begged to be put on the lists for Barry to pop around Tuesday and fill in for their slack-arsed employees.

And Barry was happy to oblige, for a fee – a large fee.

Soon he was richer than the Sultan of Brunei's big bad brother, but in the process he'd had to suffer a string of very tedious jobs that nobody else wanted to do, for good reason …

Barry's first Bludge Tuesday job placement was with the Golden Archies hamburger chain. They got onto him late one Monday afternoon, anticipating lots of sickies the following day.

They were right. Nearly nobody turned up on Tuesday except Barry, and he was immediately put onto the Golden Archies litter patrol.

The litter patrol was a very important part of the Golden

Archies operation. It was designed as one of those good corporate citizen PR gigs, and a devious plan to keep the Golden Archies in the public eye. It was, in essence, a form of free advertising for the giant greasy hamburger chain.

Barry was given a huge sack of Golden Archies hamburger wrappers and crushed thick-shake cups emblazoned with the distinctive Golden Archies logo. His job was the walk along all the roads out of town throwing the rubbish in the gutters, lobbing it in roadside shrubs, scattering it around any scenic lookouts and beauty spots, and generally making sure it could spotted along any route into town from every vantage point possible, whether the driver was in a Mini Moke or a big-rig semitrailer or a bicycle built for two.

The boss at Golden Archies explained to Barry how important it was for the customers to be reminded how much they suddenly craved a Golden Archies burger, which they would by spotting the rubbish. It was also essential for everyone to see how popular Golden Archies was with fast-food fans everywhere. The popularity of their healthy, healthy product would be judged by the amount of litter scattered around every town in Australia. That's why the chain deposited tonnes of rubbish along roadsides every day of the week, and twice a day on weekends.

Barry did it, but he felt sort of foolish. After all, most of it would end up being picked up by those meddling Clean Up Australia teams. What was the use?

Still, it wasn't Barry's job to question orders. His job, as managing director of Bludge Tuesday Employment, was to do whatever he was told on Tuesdays. So he did it, and got paid accordingly.

Barry's next Bludge Tuesday gig was with FAT, another fast-food outlet, which specialised in fried turkey. They were originally called Fried Arse Turkey, but upgraded their image to FAT to cash in on the new health-conscious fad of avoiding any reference to fried food.

Barry's job on Tuesday was to keep a constant eye on the deep-fryers and fish out all the battered rats that inevitably found their way into the production process. Serving up a bucket of fried turkeys' butts containing a battered rat was bad for business – FAT had spent a fortune changing their name to FAT, and didn't think RAT had the same far-reaching yoof-market appeal.

And anyway, their market research had told them people just weren't into eating rat's arses any more – that item went off the menu some time after the Black Death killed a few million people in Europe during the Middle Ages.

FAT didn't want to sell something that was a fad hundreds of years ago. It was bad for their image – they wanted to be a twenty-first-century operation, young, fresh, trendy and hip. There was nothing hip about rat's rings, even if the batter was good.

The other responsibility of the job at FAT was to keep loading the odour pellets into the good-smell machine, which pumped fine-food smell for a hundred metres around the FAT franchise.

The smell machine was FAT's number-one marketing toy, and a very impressive piece of machinery. The finely tuned noses of passing dudes, bombarded by the delicious smell of fried turkey, would send an order to the brain via the stomach – get in there and get me some of that fried turkey, right now!

Of course the food never tasted as good as it smelt, but whose fault was that? The good-smell machine was just another form of advertising, and everyone knows the advertising racket is so crooked that ad people can't even say 'good morning' without lying.

Barry's next Bludge Tuesday job placement was as a delivery boy for Pizza House. Their usual delivery boy, Doogle, had lost his pushie license after being busted by the police, big-time. He'd been chased by cops, doubling his girlfriend, both without helmets, and had nearly got away with it when they had a tremendous prang.

The cops put him on the blowbag, and guess what? Doogle was completely out of it! He'd consumed about fourteen schooners of red cordial, had snorted a few lines of sherbet, and ingested three cola Chuppa Chups. His blood-sugar level was through the roof, and, when questioned by the wallopers, he made even less sense than usual. He was sentenced to a hundred hours' community service, and placed in a sugar-detox program for six months. His pizza-delivery career was cactus.

Luckily for Doogle he was a good-looking rogue, and he soon got work in the beach-side soapy 'Hoax Me Away'.

But that meant Pizza House needed a new delivery boy for Tuesday, and Barry was it. Unfortunately his first delivery was nearly his last. He rocked up to the address of some party full of beautiful people, and when they answered the door they demanded to know where Doogle was.

One girl in particular, a stunner called Margaret, was so disappointed at having her dinner delivered by the rough-headed Barry that she refused to pay for the pizza, and nearly kicked him when he asked if he could lock up his bike, hang at the party, and play pool with her.

Barry decided that working Bludge Tuesday for fast-food outlets was a bad joke. After his dud experiences with the rotten-food industry, he limited his job offers to real work that didn't involve peddling crap plastic fodder.

Tuesday, and Barry he rocked up to a factory that manu-factured novelty items. That's what they told him when they made the booking over the phone, anyway. But when he arrived he found himself on the production line road-testing plastic vomits and plastic dog turds.

'How am I meant to test them?' asked Barry, a fair enough question under the circumstances.

The answer was very simple, and very wrong. Barry had to test the novelty joke items by placing them next to the real thing on the floor, closing his eyes, spinning around ten times, then poking his finger in the fake one.

If the fakes were good, then Barry shouldn't be able to tell the replicas from the real thing. That way, if Barry poked his fingers in the real spew or dog turd, the fakes were good. If not, then they had to be made again.

As you can imagine, after a day at that job Barry was nauseated and completely browned off, and it took three days to wash the smell off his hands. He vowed never to work for *that* company again.

Barry was getting heartily disillusioned. Oh sure, he'd made heaps of bread, but the job satisfaction just wasn't there. Lucky he only had to do these dud jobs on Bludge Tuesday – imagine the poor bastards that had to do them full time, all their lives. The thought disturbed Barry fully, and he resolved to give the whole gig just one more shot. The working world sucked.

Next Tuesday he got his marching orders – report to the local tourist attraction to play a colourful, high-profile character that was outrageously popular with kids and adults alike.

'That sounds more like it,' thought Barry. At last a job with some kind of status.

Well, status was one word for it. Barry was briefed on the character he was to play that Tuesday, and given his special costume. Immediately he began to have grave misgivings. Still, a job was a job, and he'd agreed to do it – he couldn't back out now.

The local tourist attraction had been modelled on those other great Aussie icons that promoted their local products by constructing a huge model as a tourist attraction – the Big Banana, the Big Pineapple, the Big Prawn, the Big Merino, the Big Trout.

As it happened, the one thing this local town had an abundance of was fat politicians. Per capita it provided more fat politicians than any other town in the country. So it seemed completely natural that they should build the Big Buttocks.

Big Buttocks stood out like a giant derriere, as you'd expect, and attracted heaps of people. They came to voice their grievances and hatred for all the lying, hypocritical politicians that ruled their country.

There was a range of games people could play to vent their spleens: throwing darts at boards with pollies' grinning mugs plastered on them; lobbing splat bombs at effigies of their craven PM; and dunking the local members of parliament into the big green gunge bucket.

But by far the most popular attraction occurred at midday, when Big Bob Buttocks came out. People formed great queues to have their go at Big Bob. They'd tell Big Bob what they hated about pollies, and Bob would nod, turn and bend over. Then they were allowed to delivery Bob the hugest, teeth-rattlingest kick in the ringpiece they could muster up.

And whose job was it to play Big Bob Buttocks on this Bludge Tuesday? You got it – Barry Roughead's. Oh, they gave him protective quoit padding and all that jazz, but you try absorbing the rage and hate-filled kicks of thousands of disgruntled voters. It wasn't fair. Barry wasn't even old enough to vote, yet he had to wear all that anger. His poor date was bruised purple, and he couldn't sit for days.

Now Barry was over it. Really over it. All the jobs he'd got through his Bludge Tuesday employment agency had been crap. Total crap. Utter crap. Complete crap. Jobwise, Barry couldn't get no satisfaction, though he tried, and he tried, and he tried, and he tried. He would've written a song about it, but he was crap at that too.

There had to be more to life than this crap existence …

So it came to pass that at the exact instant Barry Roughead turned thirteen he rocked back into school. That moment occurred in the middle of double maths. Barry stalked into the classroom, took back the bird he'd given the maths teacher, apologised to his fellow students for abusing them, and opened his maths book.

Then everything went back to normal, as if it had never changed, and Barry set about getting the best education he could. By doing that, Barry figured, he would snare some interesting and challenging job, instead of the crap employment prospects he'd had before.

The maths teacher didn't care one way or the other. She hadn't even realised Barry was missing all that time, so his return didn't make any difference to her. It was Monday, she had a bad case of the fantods, and all she had on her mind was the sickie she'd be taking tomorrow.

# Teasing Mrs Cooper

I grew up in a dusty country town with long flat roads that stretched out to nowhere and beyond. The days were unendingly long, and the nights even longer. There was nothing to do. There was nothing to talk about. There was nothing there.

That's why we'd always end up teasing Mrs Cooper.

To be completely truthful, it wasn't really Mrs Cooper we teased. She had a bad ticker. It wasn't her mother, old Mrs Cooper, either. She was a defenceless old woman with ankles like fishbones – it wouldn't have been right.

No. It was old, old Mrs Cooper we targeted – the mother of both of them. Ninety-seven years old, fully rheumatic, frail as an icicle, and blind as an oyster. Easy.

Old, old Mrs Cooper lived a couple of kilometres out of town, on her lonesome. That's where we'd always find ourselves peddling our pushies, along the rutted dirt road to her house, whenever things got dull.

We'd usually go on full moons, when there was a bit of

a wind up, and the wild dogs were howling. That's when it was easiest to get her.

We had to leave early, to get out to old, old Mrs Cooper's while she was still awake, toasting her bones by the wood-fire in the kitchen. Somehow, above the crackle of the fire and the whistling wind, she'd always hear us coming, even if we tiptoed.

It was sort of a sixth-sense thing.

She'd know something was wrong. Her hunched posture would stiffen. She'd cock her crinkled ear. Her brow would concertina into a worried frown.

Then we'd make the noise.

'*Meoow.*'

Her deeply lined face would soften into a girlish smile. We'd meow again, and she'd start to her feet, a look of childish delight in her clouded eyes. 'Tibbles? Tibbles, my darling, is that you?'

Nuh, uh. But we wouldn't discourage her.

'Meow.'

'*You're* not Tibbles. *You're* Snowdrop. Snowdrop. Snowdrop. Come on.'

Tibbles, Snowdrop, and a dozen others had been dead a dozen years. But old, old Mrs Cooper seemed to have forgotten.

That, or she thought it was their ghosts …

Either way, she'd feel her way, hand over hand, to the kitchen door, and onto the verandah. She didn't turn the light on – no need – but we'd see her dark shape move across the front of the house.

'Snowdrop.'

One of us would have brought a long stick with a wire hook bound to its end. We'd rub it on the tree branch above the verandah, trying to make it sound like a cat scratching and perching on the branch.

'*Meooow.*'

'Oh Snowdrop. You've come back to me. After so many years you're still alive! Oh, mercy be!'

'*Meeeooow.*'

'Thank you, God. Thank you! You've made a lonely old woman very happy. You're brought back, my precious pet. Oh, my darling baby.'

'Oh, my darling baby' was the cue. We'd hit the deck. You'd hear the clicks. A split-second's silence.

*Boom! Boom!*

The house would rock on its foundations! A swathe of tree would rip away with the blasts! The end of the scratch stick would be instantly shredded!

Tendrils of thick cordite smoke curled from both barrels of old, old Mrs Cooper's old, old double-barrelled shotgun.

We'd let out a long, mournful death cry.

'*Meeeeoooooooooowww-erp!*'

'Ha ha ha ha! Gotcha! Ha ha ha ha ha! Die! Mongrels!'

Old, old Mrs Cooper would cackle and caper around the verandah in delight, and do a little jig that was a cross between a war whoop and a tap dance.

Then we'd split. The shots always brought the town cop, Colin 'Ginger' Johnson. He'd hear the blasts – the whole town would. He didn't want to go out to the old lady's house, but he knew he had to. The town would be outraged if he didn't. Clearly there'd been shots fired. The old lady might be in trouble.

Ginger Johnson knew old, old Mrs Cooper wasn't in trouble. He knew what was going to happen. He knew alright. He'd wince as he pulled his big cold boots onto his bed-warmed feet. He'd feel like crying. Why him? Why, God, why? Was he a murderer in his last life? Why this constant punishment? Why this torment? Why?

Ginger would drive slowly along the dark, rutted road, sipping on a thermos of coffee. He knew he had a long ordeal in front of him. He'd arrive, kill the engine, and groan deeply as he lurched out of the cabin of his police jeep.

He'd always say the same thing. 'Mrs Cooper. It's the police.'

'The police? What do I want with the bloody police? Didn't I get enough of the bloody police being married to a bloody policeman for forty-five bloody years? Go on, git!'

'Mrs Cooper, did you discharge a firearm?'

'Yep. What of it?'

'You know you don't have a licence for that gun. You know it's illegal to discharge it in the town precinct. I could place you under arrest.'

'Bah! You couldn't arrest an unconscious wino. Anyway, it was them cats again. I bagged one. That's my thirty-fifth. Go get it for me, boy.'

That was the bit Ginger Johnson hated. Not being called 'boy' – that was nothing. It was the order to get the alleged dead cat. Ginger knew what that meant.

'Look, Mrs Cooper. There was no cat. There never *is* a cat. You're shooting at nothing.'

'Liar! Thief! You steal my cats – I know you do!'

'Mrs Cooper, I promise you I …'

'Hound! Assassin! Stealing an old lady's cats! I know you take them because I'm blind. You wouldn't dare otherwise.'

'Mrs Cooper, I do not …'

'Swineherd! Dirt! You find that cat! I bagged it. It's there alright. That's *my* cat! You find it. Now!'

Then Ginger would have to crawl around in the scrubbery with his torch, searching for a blown-away cat carcass he knew wasn't there. He didn't want to embarrass the old lady and imply she'd lost her marbles, but she really had. Ginger looked for as long as he thought it took to satisfy the old bag, then grovelled up, filthy dirty and sore.

'Mrs Cooper. There is *no* cat.'

'Scoundrel! Wretch! Villain! Rogue! *You*! I knew I couldn't trust you. All you Johnsons. All your eyes too close together. Bloody criminals, the pack of you. Always have been.'

Ginger would wince, biting his tongue. He was young enough to still care about his job. He was an officer of the law. He had to treat the inflammatory old lady with respect.

'Mrs Cooper, there is no …'

'Bah – you snake! You had plenty of time right then to steal an old blind lady's dead cat. I know. I know you take them. You're stealing them for the competition, and entering them yourself. Don't think I don't know your caper. You're planning to win the competition with *my* feral cats.'

'Mrs Cooper, I assure you, I would never …'

'Shut up! I'm charging you with theft. I'm placing you under a citizen's arrest. An old blind lady can still get justice in this country, you just wait and see if I'm wrong.'

'Mrs Cooper, don't do this, every time it's the same and it always …'

'Shut up! Get back in the jeep. You're under arrest.'

Old, old Mrs Cooper would put on her long tatty fur coat, and then she and Ginger Johnson would drive to town, in the middle of the night, in the cold, draughty police jeep. Mrs Cooper would curse the poor, hapless ginger-headed cop the whole time.

When they got to the station, Ginger would have to turn on the lights and the heater, boot up the computer, make a cup of tea for Mrs Cooper and a strong cup of coffee for himself, and register a charge of robbery against *himself*.

The whole time he'd try to talk old, old Mrs Cooper out of taking action, and she'd just back up and abuse him even more. Then he'd file the charge, print it out, write 'charge denied', and sign it. Old, old Mrs Cooper would sign it also, in her spidery old-lady handwriting, and it'd be faxed to the local court registrar.

Next morning, when the court clerk was trawling through the day's business, he'd see the charge. He'd smile wryly to himself, and dial Ginger's number.

'Got you again, did she, Ginger?'

A groan at the other end of the line was the only reply. 'What will we do with it?'

'What can we do?' whined Ginger. 'You know as well as I do there was no cat to steal. But she's adamant. I swear, the old bag's gonna send me to the nuthouse.'

'Well, we've got two choices. You can plead not guilty and it'll have to go to court, which means you have to get over to Charlatan Courthouse to face the Beak. That'll mean a day's travel both ways, and a day there in court. Plus costs and petrol money. Reckon we'd be better doing the usual. Save yourself the time and trouble and just plead guilty.'

'Yeah, Stan, I guess you're right. But blimey, this is ridiculous. I'm gonna get the sack if anyone ever gets a look at my criminal record – thirty-five charges of thieving dead cats.'

'Well, don't worry, I've put a note next to each charge, outlining the circumstances. It'll never be held against you. But if you were to front up to court and something bad happened in town while you were away, then you'd really look bad. The way I've explained it, you look like a responsible cop taking the rap for an old woman who's clearly batty.'

'Yeah, well, maybe so. But the thing that irks me is that she's in front in the competition. I tell you, that old bag hasn't potted one feral cat, yet she's credited with thirty-five kills. Thirty-five! I've only got seven, and I've hunted day and night for the mongrels. It just ain't right. She's cheating, plain as the nose on my face, rorting the justice system, and getting away with it.'

'Yep, but that's the way of the world, eh, Ginger? The law is an ass, and even though you're paid to enforce it, she's protected by it. Don't play her game – keep away from the old crow.'

'How can I? If there's shooting out there I have to go. Sure as hell the one time I don't investigate she *will* be in trouble, and the town would never forgive me.'

'Ah, the joys of being an honest cop. Oh well, must be going – duty calls.'

It was school holidays, and time was weighing heavily on our hands. There was nothing else to do, so we did it again. And again. And again.

'*Meooow.*'

'Garfield. At last. I knew you'd come back to me one day. Oh, my darling baby …'

*Boom! Boom!*

The sound of the rackety cop jeep, bouncing along the rutted road in the dead of night.

'Mrs Cooper, it's the police …'

The comp had been organised by the Australian Native Animals Protection Society, as a way to rid the area of the feral-cat menace that had nearly destroyed the local fauna.

Everyone in town had taken part with enthusiasm, trapping, poisoning and shooting every feral they could, and Ginger Johnson had been in on it up to his neck. He desperately wanted to win the thousand-dollar prize money. He'd spend whole nights out on the hunt – all for nothing.

Ginger had recorded Mrs Cooper's kills as legitimate, rather than deny her mad charges that he stole her dead cats. Though it looked ridiculous for him to admit the charge, it would have looked even more ridiculous to deny it. Nobody would have believed him. The whole Johnson clan – apart from Ginger and his mother – had a solid and completely deserved reputation in the town as thieves, rogues, and liars. Ginger was the first of the clan who'd been on the right side of the law.

But that wasn't enough. The Johnson gang's past form had tarred him with the same brush as all the others. The family rep had dragged him down. He was being punished for the whole clan's past misdeeds.

And, even though old, old Mrs Cooper didn't have a single cat carcass to verify the kills, she won the competition – on the evidence of Ginger Johnson.

Yes, pretty soon old, old Mrs Cooper 'bagged' her fiftieth cat, and won the competition hands down, at least according to the police records. Nobody else even came close to getting that many.

So old, old Mrs Cooper won the prize. Once she got the cash in her hot little hands she headed home, chuckling to herself. She rang me that night, and asked us all over for tea.

We sat around her table, sipping tea and munching scones, just like we had the night three months before when she'd first outlined her fully devious plan.

'I never knew why my Stan kept so many cats until long after it all blew over. Cats are generally pretty healthy animals – they don't get sick that often. But if you have lots of cats, well it stands to reason that there'll always be one that's sick, right? That's what Stan planned. It gave him the excuse he needed to go into town at least once a week, and visit that trollop, Beryl Johnson, the vet. They had a secret affair going, for years.

'Look at that photo. That's Stan. Now, with his red hair and freckles, who does he resemble? Anyone you know? That's right. Ginger Johnson. Ginger Johnson was his bastard son. He probably doesn't even know it. But I knew, and I always vowed to make his life hell whenever I could.'

'I never cheat – not like my husband,' she'd said. 'But you know how it is when you get old. Your brain turns to mush. You get confused easily. You can't remember things. At least that's what they tell me happens. If that's what people expect to happen, who am I to disappoint them? Since that's what they expect of old ladies, all cross-eyed confusion, I decided I might as well take advantage of it.'

And Mrs Cooper had. All she'd asked us to do was come out some nights and meow.

'Just pop out and "confuse" me,' she'd requested months before. 'I'll take care of the rest.'

We'd 'confused' her, and in the process helped Ginger to help her bag enough feral cats to win the comp. At least she *thought* she did. She *thought* she'd heard the meowing of a feral, and *thought* she'd got it with her shotgun. She was sure, as sure as an old lady can be, and at least no-one could accuse her of cheating.

'But what if it had been a real cat out there?' we asked when she gave us our half of the prize money.

'Sonny, I haven't seen a real cat round these parts since

Stan died. The day they put him in the ground I poisoned the lot of them, skinned them, dumped their carcasses on his fresh-dug grave to rot and stink to blazes, and cursed him and all his moggies to high heaven.'

She brandished her thick, tatty fur coat like a bullfighter's cape, and chuckled. 'What did you think this was made of?'

# Gordon Versus the Gourd God

The day had been no different to any other – unseasonably ordinary, inexplicably average, noteworthily eventless. Gordon Dillworthy meandered to school, zenned out in class, cruise-missiled home, swilled pumpkin soup for dinner, gawked through an hour of mind-numbing TV, crashed out hard, and racked up the zeds for roughly two hours and thirteen minutes ...

Then he died.

This event – considered serious in most societies – spiced things up, something chronic. Nobody likes waking up dead, and Gordon was no exception, though even he had to admit it turned an otherwise wastrelly day into a very important one. Only two dates made it onto a dead dude's headstone – this would be one of them.

Gordon's deathday – 7 December 1999 – would now be recorded in fresh yellow sandstone, alongside his birthday, and some sap-sucking religious verse. The elegant inscription might even make it to marble if the oldies were feeling gullible and lint-headed, and got themselves conned by the creepy funeral director into sowing the cash broadacre-style. The way that bloke leeched onto grieving customers and softly sucked them dry as a bone, the headstone would probably end up polished top-shelf marble, festooned with neon inlays, flashing frills, and a pleasing musical jingle set off by radar every time a visitor came within cooee of Gordon's decomposing remains ...

But right now Gordon didn't have time to waste thinking about those trivialities. He was dead. There was paperwork to do. He found himself in a long line, with at least a thousand disembodied ex-people in front of him. Spooky, ethereal, heaps-creepy clouds banked on the gloomy horizon, and formed menacing thunderheads in the foreground. Fringed by darkness, the sullen cloud-mass was slashed periodically with clawing bursts of incandescent lightning.

The queue of stiffs arced into Infinity. There must have been heaps of dying being done Downstairs, because it was hellishly slow going Upstairs. To make matters worse, due to staff cuts and downsizing, there were only two clerks dealing with the entire Underworld traffic. They looked older than Moses and had the vacant gaze and old-man ditheriness thing. They took forever.

It seemed like the line moved a footstep a week. The grey, spectral queuers shuffled silently forward at an agonisingly tedious pace.

Gordon waited a dog's age, fidgeting madly. He didn't like lining up for the canteen or anything, let alone this bogus rap. Jeez, he'd hardly got used to being a teenager before it was all over.

Gordon grew more and more annoyed and agitated and impatient. Finally he tapped the formless figure in front of him on its formless shoulder, or somewhere in that general direction – it was difficult to tell in the sinister half-light.

'Hey. Excuse me. What's the hold-up?'

The dead woman – for woman she once was – turned around slowly and shook her mournful head, saying nowt. The old digger behind was no help either, his hollow eyes full of mute despair and nameless dread, his mouth full of empty nothings. He wouldn't offer an answer of any kind – positive, negative, or indifferent – not even when Gordon offered him money.

Not knowing what else to do, Gordon was reduced to lurking and loafing and sighing and bitching and generally waiting his turn. He made a mental note to thoroughly up whoever was in charge of the show. Even the school canteen handled crowd control better than this …

'This is a bloody disgrace!' snorted Gordon when he finally reached the front of the line. 'This is a *joke*! I've been waiting for hours! *Days*! Who's in charge here? What's the go? This setup *sucks*!'

The grizzled clerk examined his gnarly fingernails, apparently oblivious to the *gravitas* of Gordon's grievances. He leant forward, gripping a clump of his flowing white beard, and proceeded to shine a dull spot on his huge pearly desk in an irritatingly nonchalant manner. The far north regions of his long, wizened face sported two bushy, hairy, white, out-of-control eyebrows, which now came right down to drink as he frowned deeply, sighed like an airbag in an accident, and murmured …

'Name?'

'Gordon Dillworthy … and *I* want answers. Why in Hell's name does it take …'

'Address, Dillworthy?'

'Forty-four Beaconbum Road, Sandalsoap … and let me tell you, we don't tolerate this sort of shabby inefficiency there, not when it …'

The clerk flipped casually through a huge papyrus ledger, completely oblivious to Gordon's whining. He hummed periodically, studiously ignoring the dead kid for the full duration of his rant.

The ancient man's hooked finger finally came to rest on a long and detailed entry in the far left-hand column. His crackly lips silently mouthed words as he read the confidential client information. Then he began to slowly shake his snowy mane, with what started as indignation but quickly escalated to boiling red outrage.

'Well might you mention Hell in your ignorant ravings, Low One – that is, indeed, your destination!'

'Eh?'

'Hell, my foul-featured young simian, is your new and endless address.'

'Say *what?* Why? What's the score? Why me?'

'Why you? *Why you?* Why do you think, infidel? You have dedicated your short and brutish life to degrading, debasing, destroying and desecrating the Supreme Being. You have even …' (here the clerk broke down in blithering anger) '… you have even – oh, I can hardly say it – you have even *eaten* our Holy Creator. Regularly. But oh, oh, *now* you will burn, Low One. Burn! Hot! Ouch! Not just for an afternoon, either, son-of-seven-devils! No. You'll burn for Eternity!'

'What are you talking about, *eaten?* I haven't eaten anybody.'

'No body, maybe, but our Glorious Creator nonetheless. And its many, many offspring and relatives. Oh, you're for it, big boy. *Really* for it.'

'You're insane. I haven't done anything wrong. I'm just a normal kid. There's heaps of evil low-lifes down there – why not take one of them?'

'Oh, we'll take them alright, don't you worry about that – we'll take them all. But first we'll take *you*. Oh, there'll be some celebrating here tonight, let me tell you. You're a rare catch – you're on our Most Wanted list.'

'*What!* What for?'

'What *for?* Need you ask, Low One? For mass murder ...'

Gordon Dillworthy, mass murderer. Serial killer. Filthy, cowardly, cold-blooded deathmeister. It didn't sound right – but it was all true. And Gordon wasn't the only one. Out of the entire crowd of dead types milling around waiting to be sorted and yarded at the pearly desks, only two *weren't* murderers. Two, out of at least a thousand. Nearly everyone was guilty, and going to Hell ...

It couldn't happen? Impossible? Wildly improbable? You be the judge.

Religion – nothing but trouble, right? Right, because most religions got it wrong. Sure, they sounded pretty solid with their 'thou shalt nots' and 'do unto undies' sort of talk, but underneath the incense and threats and bluster they were talking one hundred per cent footrot. Big-brand bugaboo, by the bundle.

All the serious players got it wrong – dead wrong – and in the final wash-up there were Christians, Buddhists, Muslims, Jews, Jains, Zoroastrians, even the groovy Rastas. They were *all* duds. They'd all claimed there was only one true Creator, and they were right – but *theirs* wasn't it. They'd all backed the wrong horse with the cloven-footed bookie, and soon they'd be required to pay up on their losing bets – big-time.

Suckers.

The only religion that actually got it right was an extremely obscure cult of genuine, warp-speed, seed-sucking freaks who worshipped, as their living deity and Glorious Creator, the pumpkin.

The Great Pumpkin – according to their flaky, esoteric literature – had created the world in seven growing seasons. On the eighth it squatted back to admire its hydra-headed handiwork.

Its many millions of vines and tendrils had spread and multiplied to form the leafy green universe, with the planet Earth as its favourite compost heap. The very finest pumpkins grew on Earth – but they also died on earth.

A truly barbaric race had grown to dominate the Earth, and in turn dominate the sacred pumpkin. The Killing Times began. Humans grew mighty fond of the taste of pumpkin flesh, and devised a thousand cunning ways to trap, kill, and cook the good-tasting gourd.

It was a fully treacherous scene, pumpkinwise.

The truth of the Great Pumpkin was known to few, and followed by even fewer. The spinner who drew the Charlie Brown comic strip 'Peanuts' was one. He tried to warn the world through the lettuce-limp character Linus, who dragged a security blanket around and every Halloween waited in the pumpkin patch for the Coming of the Great Pumpkin.

But Linus wasn't enough. Most people dismissed him as a wet wuss, and the worship of the Great Pumpkin as trumped-up, brimstone-reeking, heathen juju. Humans went right on merrily growing and slaughtering pumpkins, and worshipping graven images with bizarre ceremonies, in defiance of the Great Pumpkin's teachings.

As it was, the only thing any of these heathen human religions got right was the name of the patch where the Great Pumpkin grew, where the souls heading for salvation blissed out for Eternity. Even then they spelt it wrong.

The correct spelling was Hea*vine* ...

Well. All this was news to Gordon – grim, ugly, rancid, el grimmo, deeply disturbing, nauseatingly negative news. Because not only had Gordon eaten pumpkins in a million different dishes, but he'd also slaughtered a billion more before their time. That was a conservative estimate – it could've been more.

Now he was busted. Badly.

See, Gordon's yard backed onto old Chesterton's vast

pumpkin patch. Old Chesterton grew prizewinning pumpkins, and was himself a prizewinning pain in the passage.

Old Chesterton loved his great orange pumpkins like treasures. Exhibited them in shows all over the country. Won the Royal half a dozen times. He was loopy for those conspicuously coloured cucurbits.

Never did a man love a vegetable like old Chesterton, mainly because he was cranky in the head, but also because his real life was so empty. Big pumpkins filled that gap, and, kilo for kilo, delivered more happiness to his delicate little heart than any single thing he'd ever experienced.

As if the father wasn't bad enough, the apelike son, Cyril, was infinitely worse. Cyril Chesterton's tastes were simple. He was not a complex boy. He liked nothing more than watching violent videos, studying the real action in slomo frame-by-frame sequence, then road-testing the most dangerous and radical moves on his neighbour, Gordon Dillworthy.

Cyril watched a *lot* of videos. He had a lot of dangerous and radical moves to get through. He made full use of his smaller, weedier neighbour's very close proximity, regarding the Dillworthy backyard as his gym, and Gordon as his personal punching bag.

Every opportunity – whether Gordon needed it or not – Cyril hurdled the back fence and beat his favourite neighbour like a glue-sniffing mule.

It didn't seem right ...

But Gordon got the Chestertons back, in a big way. He'd exacted his revenge surreptitiously, ambushing old Chesterton's prize pumpkins and then coldly, calculatingly, serially killing them. He'd wait for the Chesterton family to slither off to church each Sunday, then practise target-shooting over the fence with his sure-shot shit-hot slingshot.

Gordon could have really taken advantage of a situation like this. He could have gone mental. But he didn't – he wasn't heartless. He knew how much time, effort, love and money old Chesterton put into his pumpkin patch. He knew how many drudgerous hours Cyril had been press-ganged into helping dig, manure, mulch, plant, weed and water that vast pumpkin patch.

Gordon knew all these things. He took them all into due consideration. He wasn't *that* low – he would never have laid waste to the whole lot. He would never have shot *all* of Chesterton's pumpkins.

Just the biggest and best ones.

Gordon used tiny steel ball-bearings as ammo. The wound was invisible even to old Chesterton's highly trained eye, but within a week the tiny hole went cancerous, and gangrenous, and scrofulous, and the pumpkin died from the inside out in a stinking frenzy of pus-orange slop, not to mention extremely mysterious circumstances.

It was *wrong*.

When old Chesterton discovered each new loss he'd curse and cry and carry on like a sick-headed, south-bound sailor soused and shanghaied in Singapore. Why was it always the best pumpkins that carked it, the ones Chesterton knew would hammer the opposition in any pumpkin comp from here to Humpty Doo? It wasn't fair, goddamnit!

Old Chesterton would perform weeping autopsies over the beloved vegetables, vowing to God to *destroy* whatever pest, insect, rodent or feral critter was persecuting his pumped-up prizewinners. Then he'd spray forty different brands of deadly poisons all over the patch, toxing out the area for generations.

But his big pumpkins kept on dying …

'You killed, in cold blood, twenty-two thousand one hundred and three bright, hopeful, ambitious young pumpkins, at last count … which *is* the last count, Low One.'

Gordon was dumbfounded. He swallowed heavily. He felt squeamish inside, sweaty outside, and gravel-gutted in the parts in between. He swallowed heavily, again.

'But h-how was I to know? Nobody told *me* pumpkins were special. Nobody said anything about anything,' Gordon weaselled.

'Ignorance is no defence, infidel. Your blood-drenched past lies behind you, Dillworthy, and your horrible Fate before you. Behold, Dillworthy! Hell! Your home *forever!*'

The old man flourished dramatically with his left arm, and, with a squawk, tumbled backwards off his cheapo swivel chair. The backdrop of cloudbanks fell, piling into a heap – it had actually been an exceedingly well-painted canvas backdrop, just like in the big-budget movies. Some Hollywood special-effects feller had died, and the PR bigwigs in Heavine were making good use of his skill and artistry, for dramatic presentations.

And it couldn't have got more dramatic than this. Scattered across a gigantic, smoke-hazed battlefield were a thousand thousand different pots, pans, skittles, boilers, steamers and cookers of every description, heating over slow fires. Writhing in each cooking receptacle like retarded roundworms were screaming humans, being basted and prodded and seasoned and occasionally sampled by swarms of shadowy cooks, wielding red-hot tridents and rough wooden spoons.

'We have perfected many thousands of scrumptious human recipes,' cackled the fossily clerk, 'as many as there are recipes for pumpkin. More maybe. Now *you* will be cooked forever, Dillworthy. Your punishment will be slow, and endless, and excruciatingly painful in every conceivable way. But, on the bright side, you get to choose the recipe. We're more than fair here – you decide how you'll be cooked for the rest of time. Just between you and me, don't choose the kebab …'

'But, but … Jeez, I don't want any of them. I don't want to be cooked, I've done nothing wrong. I've, I've … wait! I know. This is all a bad dream. I'll wake in a few hours and laugh about this weirdery.'

'Laugh? You will never laugh again, Dillworthy. Your arse is grass, it's mown, and the clippings are about to hit their last compost heap. This is real, you are dead, and Hell is your new holiday destination – *forever!*'

Just then – when all seemed lost – the hairy gent at the pearly desk got a top-line priority call on the greenphone. A thick pumpkin tendril curled snakily up to the clerk's scabrous, wrinkly ear, while another rose to form the tightly spiralled mouthpiece of the vinephone. He listened, intently.

The incoming info slowly logged onto the old dude's shipboard computer. The crumblie clerk blanched as white as his beard when the shock new facts legged it from his ear to his brain. He was speaking to the Great Pumpkin Itself!

He fell to his knees in awe, mumbling grovelly phrases of worship and obsequiousness to the Pumpkin God. Then, as he listened, he rose in humble protest and sat back heavily into his unstable seat.

'But ... but he is one of the worst yet, Great One ... yes, but he is completely evil in every way, a villain of the deepest dye, a scoundrel of the worst stamp, and probably a card-carrying ... yes, Great One. Yes. Yes, my Lord. Yes, Your Portly Pumpkinness. Thy will be done.'

The pumpkin tendrils withdrew as silently as they'd appeared, and the clerk rubbed his furrowed forehead. He was perplexed, bewildered and flummoxed, looking like he'd just lost the best fish *ever* off his hook.

'I don't understand this at all. It seems you've been granted a conditional reprieve – on certain *very* strict conditions.'

Just like a dog with a detonator driven up its date, Gordon knew the situation was deadly dire. His head nearly fell off nodding with instant and very vigorous agreement. 'What conditions? *What?* I'll do *anything* to slide south of this dodgy setup.'

'Are you familiar with a man called Charles Winston John Howard Chesterton?'

'Old Chesterton? Yeah – he's my back neighbour. He's a real mean mother ...'

'Then it appears to be your lucky day, Dillworthy. Geographical circumstance, and the divine grace of the Supreme Creator, have conspired to give you a second chance. If it was up to me I'd boil your head harder than a breakfast egg, mince your torso through a rusty meat grinder, marinate your kidneys in aromatic herbs, fry your ribs in emu grease, broil your butt over red-hot hickory coals, mash your brains into dip with sour cream and chives, and grind your lips, nose, earlobes and digits into a continental-style stuffing, a bready–crumby sort of affair, to serve on the side. All of which would set off beautifully my special flamenco-inspired flaming-ring rissoles. Then, *bon appétit,* as they say on the Continent.

'But, alas, it is not to be. You have *one* chance, Low One. This Chesterton fellow is growing a pumpkin – a *very* special pumpkin. He has erected a perspex barrier around this pumpkin, to protect it from vermin like you. He plans to enter it in the local pumpkin-growers' competition, then carve it into a jack-o'-lantern for Halloween. Such a barbaric custom …

'This pumpkin is not your stock-standard, straight-eight gourd, Low One. Its divine vine traces directly back to the Supreme Creator. That pumpkin is actually the Son of God, spawned from the Great Pumpkin's divine seed. It cannot be allowed to die. It *must not* die. You, Dillworthy, know the layout. You know this old Chesterton heathen. You must save the Son of God. Do not fail, Infidel. If you *should* fail … well, you've seen Hell's Kitchen. You will be the next savoury dish. Your call, soul of a swineherd.'

'I'll do it. No sweat. I'll do it. It'll be easy.'

Easy is easy to say, another thing to do. Gordon woke with a shudder. He was back in his bedroom – his beloved, familiar, childhood bedroom that stank of dirty rotten socks and hidden, decomposing bananas. Deep and boundless joy! It *had* been a dream.

Gordon coughed to clear his morning throat, and a shower of pumpkin seeds shot out of his gob like spray from a whale spout. He went through the standard waking-up groan drill, but didn't hear any noise – his earflaps were stuffed solid with seed. His nostrils, both channels, were jammed chockers with slimy, snot-covered seeds. His undies were full, too.

No. It hadn't been a dream. It was real. It was a warning – and not just about the dangers of wearing undies to bed.

It was Gordon's last and only chance not to go to Hell …

Old Chesterton was most definitely unaware he was growing the Son of God in his backyard suburban pumpkin patch, but nevertheless sensed he was onto some king-size, hell-special, butt-kicking, supercharged species of vegetable.

The monstrous thing had put on a phenomenal growth spurt within days of germinating, pumping like no pumpkin ever. At night it seemed to glow and throb, generating its own thin halo of incandescent white light.

The pumpkin grew and grew. After a fortnight it was the size of a basketball. After a month it was bigger than an earthball.

The big, beautiful pumpkin was like a holy revelation for old Chesterton. It meant that for the first time ever, in his whole miserable life, he wouldn't have to cheat. Usually Chesterton's biggest and best specimens were no bigger and better than other competitors', and he'd had to inject vegetable steroids or sew lumps of lead into the base to tip the scales in the final weigh-in.

But not with this pumpkin. No, sir. Its massively huge rotundity was beyond anything old Chesterton had ever seen, or read of in his dreary pumpkin-grower's magazines, or even conceived of in his most dubious dreams. Knowing he'd surely win – without having to cheat in any way – made old Chesterton feel proud and pious and holy and pure, like the Lamb of God.

He wasn't, of course. Like the Buddha reckoned, it was all an illusion. Old Chesterton was just a crusty, creepy, hypocritical bigot, with a very big pumpkin.

He may have been all bad, but Old Chesterton did know when he was onto a good thing. And he knew – sure as he'd been born backwards – that he'd be a legend in pumpkin circles for this boomer.

To protect his prize pumpkin from the mysterious local pumpkin scourge, old Chesterton constructed a perspex structure over the hallowed site. He rigged it out with tubes and feeders and hi-techo Death Star gadgetry. He force fed the orange mega-beast with vitamin sprays and shots of carbon dioxide and $H_2O$, along with a million pills and powders and lotions and potions. He even sang his favourite churchy hymns to it, until its tendrils started wilting.

Old Chesterton had lost a lot of pumpkins to the elusive local pumpkin killer. Too many pumpkins. Now he was being heaps careful. He was determined not to lose this big sucker, and spent mondo cash protecting it.

He rigged out a radar alarm system, pit-traps like the hillbillies use on their marijuana crops, and sound-sensitive security lights. He dug moats and rigged tripwires. He hung protective voodoo dolls in the trees above. Pretty soon old Chesterton had his backyard stitched up tighter than an unacclimatised kipper's clavicle ...

When Gordon sussed the pumpkin patch first thing that first morning born again, he instantly knew he was in a *lot* of trouble. The potential for a straightforward pumpkin abduction seemed slim at best, and blatantly, obviously, ridiculously impossible at worst.

The divine vege in question wasn't difficult to spot. It stood out like a beacon light, busting bright orange, throbbing with rampant growing energy, and though Gordon was relieved to see the pumpkin looked healthy, hoopy and in every way happy, that was where the good vibe ended. The spot in the patch where the Son of God huddled was not only impenetrable, but downright dangerous.

To steal the pumpkin out of the backyard would've required serious equipment, which Gordon didn't have. He knew he couldn't lift the whopping vegetable by himself, and getting any sort of machinery into Chesterton's backyard without setting off the guard dogs was not a happening action.

Gordon didn't even know *what* he was supposed to do with the orange beast once he finally got hold of it. All he knew was this; if he didn't want to go back to Hell, and cook in his own juices forever, he had to save that holy pumpkin from the chop. Everything else would take care of itself.

So he reckoned …

A week passed. Gordon spent it hiving around frantic, as though every day was his last. When he wasn't revising and re-revising his Great Pumpkin Plan, he was warning all his mates and family and anyone who'd listen not to eat any more pumpkins. Ever again.

Community service goes woefully unrewarded in our modern society, but dire warnings of death from above or the world ending on Tuesday usually pull a crowd and get a half-decent hearing. Especially if you really shout it out.

Gordon stood on a street corner next to the bloke with 'The World Will End on Tuesday' sign, and spread the word of the Great Pumpkin. He shouted passionately, with true fear in his heart, and drew an excellent crowd, which looked like being swayed his way. For a while anyway.

But then someone in the throng released the rumour that Gordon was anti-vegetable all round – a ranting vegetablist, a paid agent of the meat industry.

Suddenly everything turned bad. Gordon got howled down, pelted with drink bottles, and beaten insensible by a hairy rabble of rabid vegetarians, professional agitators, and a safari-suited businessman hocking back a greasy dagwood dog. The rest of the crowd, including some of Gordon's best mates, stood by laughing and hooting.

The whole week was a hellbroth of public embarrassment for Gordon. But pretty soon it was the weekend, and the Sandalsoap Show was in full swing.

Old Chesterton moved his amazing vegetable on the back of a truck, and parked it at the showground on Saturday morning. Everyone was astounded at its amazing dimensions, and old Chesterton glowed with pride.

The pumpkin competition entries were viewed by the public Saturday arvo, and judged Sunday morning by a panel of expert pumpkinheads.

The winner was to be carved into a gruesome charity jack-o-lantern and carted up to the kids hospital, to scare the young patients better. From the start it was obvious who the winner was going to be – the immense, astounding, and in every way impressive Son of God, old Chesterton's vege.

First prize to Chesterton, last prize to Gordon. The pumpkin would be slaughtered and sculptured and die now, sure as, plummeting Gordon into Hell for eternity.

Even at that moment the vegetable sculptors were marking out the slash lines in chalk, gently so as not to rock the immense gourd as it teetered on the high winner's pedestal. When they'd marked out the grimacing face, one began sharpening the long, cruel butcher's scimitar necessary for the job. That was the blade the tall sculptor would use to do the fine detail work. His mate, the fat fella, took care of the rough stuff with a chainsaw, which he now fuelled up ready for the task ahead – to hack the guts out of the Son of God.

Suddenly the crowds around the sculptors parted with howls of dismay. Two dogs had escaped from the dog-show enclosure and, having eyed each other favourably and gone through the appropriate bum-sniffing formalities, decided that the middle of the crowd was the best place around to go at it, hammer and tongs.

There's no need to get into technicalities, but when the two love-crazed canines had quit their cupidous capering they found themselves glued, butt to butt, unable to bear the pain of separation. Love hurts, and this fact was duly demonstrated by the two hounds as they howled and whimpered, trying to tear apart.

Some blushing people didn't know where to look. Other people showed them where by pointing and howling with laughter. The pumpkin-comp organiser ran off to get a bucket of water, and old Chesterton put his hands over Cyril Chesterton's eyes, and closed his own to avert them from the unholy spectacle.

Gordon saw his chance. God knows he knew what he did was wrong, but the choices were few, and the options ugly. With an almighty heave, he pushed at the monstrous pumpkin perched on the pedestal.

The huge thing wobbled one way and then the other, slowly rocking with the momentum of its weight, and the pedestal rocked with it. Forward and back it heaved, before gravity took a hand. With a great rush of wind, and a huge black shadow like the sun had gone behind a cloud permanently, the pumpkin plummeted.

Old Chesterton never knew what hit him. Cyril Chesterton, if he'd had a moment to reflect on the impact, probably would have thought Jackie Chan had hit him. *Thuuuump!* A crash, a bounce, and the great pumpkin landed on its two surrogate parents with an enormous *whack!*

It crushed them flatter than horseflies, then carved a path through the terrified crowd like the rolling round rock in *Raiders of the Lost Ark*.

Gordon sprinted after it. It was heading straight for the Ferris wheel. It got there in seconds, rolling straight over the barrier and into a car, knocking the Ferris wheel bloke for six, and hitting the terminal-velocity switch on the control panel.

The great wheel fired up. It began to turn, faster and faster. Steam and sparks belted out of the engine. Then, momentarily, everything when silent. Time and sound froze in a vacuum. In clipped slow-motion the huge wheel seized, stopped dead, and flicked the massive orange pumpkin out like a stone from a catapult.

The holy pumpkin soared for the stars like a streak and, just before Gordon lost sight of it, disappeared in a burst of pure light energy …

Gordon had a dream that night. He was in the interminable line again, with the dithering old dudes processing death applications, but this time he was in the VIP section. He didn't have to wait at all. Within seconds of arriving he was whisked away from the crowds, and ushered through a gold door.

He found himself in a vast, never-ending, impossibly green and luxuriant pumpkin patch. There, squatted in the centre of a green vine throne, radiating energy and calm at the same time, was the last word in ginormous pumpkins. It spoke telepathically.

'You have done well, Earthling. You saved my boy. In light of this magnificent gesture, I am prepared to pardon you for the many nefarious atrocities you have committed upon me, and my divine creations.'

'Um, thanks. Heaps.'

'But know this, Dillworthy. No more pumpkins. Your number's up. I've got my good eye on you. If you dare to eat or kill pumpkin again, there'll be no getting away from the long vine of vengeance.'

'Yeah, I hear you. No worries. I'll never touch it again. It'll be easy.'

Easy is easy to say, another thing to do. Old habits die hard. Pumpkin had always been the number one grub-site on Gordon Dillworthy's fodder-wide-web, before his dramatic conversion. But, difficult as it was, he stuck to his promise. No more pumpkin.

Gordon lived a long, relieved and happy life, never touching pumpkin again, and strongly advising others not to do so either. He ate other stuff, growing particularly fond of one brand of frozen vegetable pies. It tasted very pumpkiny but didn't list pumpkin in its ingredients at all. It helped Gordon withdraw from eating pumpkins, which, until his first death, had been a mealtime mainstay. The delicious vege pies filled that yawning gap.

Gordon was blissfully unaware that the elderly woman on the labelling line at the frozen-food factory was illiterate, cross-eyed, dyslexic, drank booze for breakfast, didn't know left from right, and almost constantly mixed up the labels on the vege pie and pumpkin pie. She did her best, but nearly always got it wrong.

How on earth was Gordon to know?

He wasn't – but he'd find out soon enough …

# The Crappy Filler
# Story

Stick Barrett, the normally calm and generally half-sane Pants on Fire editor, came barrelling into Pants on Fire HQ, waving his arms like a demented robot and growling like a gorilla with its goolies gripped in a garbage grinder.

'Red alert! Big panic! Five Bells! Hold the presses! Doom and destruction!' he howled, ashen-faced and mealy-mouthed and glassy-eyed and bollocky-voiced.

'What's wrong with you?' asked shonky in-house author Paul Stafford, even though he wasn't interested. He was examining his grimy toenails, trying hard to gauge whether they were due for their annual clip, trim and buff.

'What's wrong? *What's wrong?* Everything's wrong, that's what's wrong. *Everything!*'

'So what's new?' asked Stafford in a sarky voice.

'What's gonna be new is your address, sunshine. We're in big trouble, and unless you can fix it, you're new address is going to be Bathurst Gaol, also known as the Big House, otherwise known as the Can, man.'

'What are you gibbering about, you bantering buffoon? What have *I* done?'

'What *haven't* you done, don't you mean. *You* haven't written enough stories. We've run out of stories. We're going to be short of stories. There aren't enough pages in *Totally Toasted.*'

Stafford sprang to life like an electrified roo. 'Jesus Jones! Christ on a crutch! Hell in a handbasket! What are we going to do?'

'What do you mean "we", white man? What are *you* going to do? You're in it up to your neck. If that book's shorter than a hundred pages, those kids are going to string you up by the nuts, and whatever's left will be tossed in the clink for false advertising. You know how obsessed kids are these days about getting value for money. They warned you last time – this time they'll chew you up and spit you out like fried tofu chunks.'

Stick chortled evilly to himself. Secretly he was pleased to see Stafford in such a terrifying pickle. If the halfwit writer was knocked off his perch this time, Stick would have first dibs on the swanky office chair he'd been coveting for the last six months, the one Stafford flatly refused to share.

The chair was worth a king's ransom, and Stafford wouldn't part with it, not even for a second.

'No way,' Stafford had said when Stick begged to just sit in it for five minutes, to experience its pure ergonomic plushness. 'It's formed in the shape of my butt – your misshapen ringpiece will throw it completely out of whack.'

But now it seemed that Stick would get his revenge on the recalcitrant Pants on Fire writer, at last. And then he'd get the chair.

Sweet.

Stafford had broken into a terminal sweat when he learnt they were one story short. His head was in his hands. His hands were in his lap. His butt was in his chair.

'What am I going to do?' he moaned aloud, pathetically.

General George, the office heavy of Pants on Fire HQ, drifted into the scene.

'What's wrong with that fool?' he asked Stick, nodding over at the blubbering mess that used to be part human, but now resembled a sack of unrecycled rubbish.

'Stafford hasn't written enough stories to fill *Totally Toasted*,' answered Stick. 'He's run out of ideas – and brain cells. We're about to go to press, and he's doomed. Ha ha.'

'Can't he just steal one of Paul Jennings' ideas, like he usually does?' asked General George.

'No dice,' answered Stick. 'He's already flogged about seven hundred ideas from him, and Paul Jennings has promised he'll sue our butts so severely there'll be nothing left to wipe.'

'Heavy,' murmured George. 'And I always thought Paul Jennings was such a decent, pleasant chap.'

'He *is* a decent, pleasant chap – salt of the earth,' affirmed Stick. 'But a man can only be pushed so far.'

'I guess so,' agreed George, but brightened up suddenly. 'Hey – I know. Do another story about the Golden Archies hamburger chain. You know, something really *off*, like how they have a pet cemetery out the back and mush up all the dog and cat carcasses to use in their burgers.'

'We can't – Charley Archie has already sent hired thugs around to warn us off. After that last story when Golden Archies employed kids with flu so they could use their phlegm as a thick-shake base, they've run out of patience too. Plus he says if we keep making a big deal about them sacking kids when they turn eighteen so they don't have to pay above-slave wages, he'll sue us for every red cent we have.' Stick shook his head with grim finality. 'No, I think we've pushed the Golden Archies people about as far as we can. You've made too many enemies in this town, Stafford. There's nobody left to write about.'

'Well, maybe he could write something about us,' said George.

'Like what?' blubbered Stafford, his face still smothered in his hands.

'Like how cool it is to be a writer, what a rad life it is, how funky the whole gig is, big bucks, fame and fortune, fast cars, rock n' roll! Goin' off! Yeah!'

'Are you serious?' asked Stafford, raising his tear-streaked face. 'I don't even have enough money to buy new undies. And all I can afford to eat for lunch is second-hand greasy chips.'

'Well that will never do,' said General George. 'You'll just have to lie. Any kid lamebrained enough to read the rubbish you write will fall for just about any story. Write how you eat canapes and truffles for lunch, every day.'

'Aren't canapes the things that keep the sun off your house?' asked Stafford.

'And isn't truffles that horrible stuff your granny makes out of leftover jelly bits and stale cake?' asked Stick.

'You're a pair of uncultured clowns,' snapped General George, scornfully. 'You're thinking of canopies and trifle. Canapes are fine French pancakes and truffles are very expensive fungi that grow underground. Shows what you ignorami know.'

Then Jarrod McCauley sauntered into the office. Officially he was the Pants on Fire troubleshooter, but in reality he was the Pants on Fire troublemaker. He was fresh from making some trouble, somewhere. 'Smells like somebody died in here. And why all the long faces – as the vet said to the racehorses.'

'Because Stafford has screwed up. He's one story short. And we're about to go to the printers,' answered Stick, scarcely bothering to hide the glee in his voice at Stafford's dire predicament.

'Well,' ruminated Jarrod, 'why don't you write a story about writing a story. Like, a story about how this really ugly stupid writer dude was one story short, and they were about to publish the book, and he couldn't think what to write …'

'Hey!' said Stafford, sparking up for the first time. 'That's a great idea, Big J. Sort of an allegoric story.'

'Isn't that one of those bendy curves in mathematics?' asked Jarrod. 'You know, an allegoric curve.'

Stafford snorted disdainfully. 'That's a parabolic curve. Dunce!'

Jarrod leapt the desk, ready to deck the pesky writer. 'Why you …'

But Stafford was too quick. He bravely and courageously defended himself by grabbing a pair of glasses he kept beside his computer for just such a dangerous situation. He jammed them on his face.

'You wouldn't hit a man with glasses, would you?' he whimpered.

'Bah … you loser!' Jarrod turned on his heels and rocked out. He had bigger fish to fry.

'I think Jarrod's onto it,' said General George. 'That's the best idea – go the true-life angle. Write a story about a story. Start with what you did on the weekend, when you thought the books were completed, how you kicked back in truly magnificent style.'

'Yeah. OK,' said Stafford. 'It was a hell of a weekend, let me tell you. While the Porsche warmed up, my girlfriend – a high-profile TV celeb – and I packed a swanky picnic basket full of high-price nibblies, fed my racehorse, sent a few e-mails to my agents in London, New York and Paris, and then hit the road. Those greed-head agents were desperate keen to get me locked into some filthy circuit of ritzy tours, but I knocked them back, even though they were talking seven figures …'

Tony Crawford, the big kahuna, came bumbling in. 'Hey – good news. We miscalculated on the page count. It's fine. The book's full. You don't have to write any more of that worthless gibberish.'

Stafford breathed a sigh of genuine relief.

'To hell with this,' he muttered, and hit the kill switch on his computer.

'Please can I sit in your chair?' wheezled Stick.

'Bugger off!' barked Stafford.

'What did you *really* do on the weekend?' asked General George.

Stafford shrugged. 'Nuthin.'